A TANK...AND A TEAM

The tank was beat up, full of holes, with more scars than a punch-drunk fighter on a barn circuit. But the crew gave her the kind of affection fighting men feel for good machinery. They called her Daisy, and they were willing to ride her to Hell and back. And their mission was a hellish one. The strike force was strictly a distraction, meant to gain time and confuse the enemy. If Daisy brought them out alive, they'd be ready to retire her with honors. For the Germans were sweeping forward powerfully, and they'd be lucky not to be pinned down and blown to shrapnel. Certainly, they had enough problems without the festering feud between Colonel Hagen and Sergeant Dixon . . .

KILLER TANK

NORMAN DANIELS

PRESTIGE BOOKS · NEW YORK

KILLER TANK

First edition March 1965
Second edition March 1969

PRESTIGE BOOKS INC. • 18 EAST 41ST STREET
NEW YORK, N.Y. 10017

ONE

Bill Freeman squinted through the command periscope, studying the hedgerow. It looked like all the others which they'd stormed, blasted and fought through ever since D-Day.

The tank was buttoned up. Fifty yards to the right squatted *Dandy*, an exact replica of Sergeant Freeman's Medium Sherman tank. Above, one of the small observation planes dipped and soared and passed on information which was being transmitted to Sergeant Freeman. Behind this hedgerow was a farmhouse and several outbuildings. They looked innocent enough to the observer riding safely high above. To a tanker, any farmhouse meant heavy German armor lurking behind it, too well camouflaged for an air observer to spot. Or an anti-tank gun, or a squad of Krauts with one of their damned *Panzerfausts*.

Every hedgerow was a fort which had to be taken one by one and Sergeant Freeman and *Daisy* had taken many of them. He'd seen armor blown to hell about as many times as they'd cut through the hedgerows. *Daisy* had taken half a dozen shells squarely on her lumpy, sand-bagged nose and weathered them, but there was always the chance of a gun, well-placed and hidden, to get a Sherman silhouetted and crashed an 88 through the weakly-armored sides.

Mike Amory was at the 75 mm gun. His loader, Sal Monda, waited in his usual sweat of anticipation. Terry Kiley in the bog seat, sighted his .50 calibre machine gun with his finger on the trigger and the box of ammo ready to feed the heavy slugs in deadly numbers, until the belt was exhausted.

Rod Carter was the driver, peering through his periscope, foot set to tread heavily on the gas. The Wright engines ran smoothly on high octane. Everything was set.

Sergeant Freeman picked up the radio mike. He used the day's code. "Commander Tuesday Four. Come in Tuesday Four."

The radio squawked. "Tuesday Four, we're set."

Freeman kicked Carter lightly and the tank began to move out. Freeman's periscope revealed the thin line of engineers beginning to move out ahead of the tanks.

"Terry . . . open up," Freeman commanded.

The bow gun began to pound. Heavy slugs slashed through the brush on top of the hedgerow. Sweeping the fire steadily, Terry Kiley held down any Krauts who might have opened up on the engineers.

Dandy was in action too, taking care of the north sector of the hedgerow. Dirt, bark, leaves, all were blasted clear. Sergeant Freeman ducked his head slightly to shout at the gunner.

"Mike . . . put one through straight ahead."

The 75 kicked, the shell casing bounced out of the breech. Sal Monda slammed an A-P in its place. The H-E drilled a hole through the hedgerow and the

6

engineers moved up, running clumsily with their loads of explosives.

Dandy drilled a second hole not far from the one Mike Amory had blasted out. The engineers converged on these while the machine guns on the tanks kept up a steady barrage of hot steel against the top of the rows.

The engineers had little to do but thrust their explosive charges into the holes, set the fuses and get the hell out of there. They gave themselves time to retreat behind the tanks. Now the doughs were scrambling to their feet, getting ready to follow the tanks. Four of them crawled onto the mud-smeared back of *Daisy*, others fell in behind.

The explosive charges went off with a roar, huge sections of the hedgerow seemed to lift right off the earth and settle back as mud and loose dirt, leaving a gaping hole in the hedgerow through which a tank could pass without lifting its soft belly high into the air for the benefit of some anti-tank gunner.

Now the farm was revealed to them as *Daisy* waddled on through. It was closely followed by *Dandy* and, once clear of the hedge, *Dandy* caught up to go forward on a line with her mate.

Sergeant Freeman wetted his lips. He could feel the sweat beading under his armpits. He was a real sweater and he should have stopped worrying long ago, because he'd taken so many of these hedgerows and what lay behind them, that the operation should have been routine. But nothing is routine when war is involved. He'd found that out too.

The farmhouse was untouched. A barrage had been laid down and some of the outbuildings were blown to hell, but the red-roofed house stood there like the Rock of Gibraltar, defying them. Freeman remembered one of these innocent looking farmhouses which some enterprising Kraut engineers had rigged up. The whole wall fell away and one of their heavies had waddled out, its 88 rifle drilling holes in the Shermans unlucky enough to be within its range.

Freeman himself had seen plenty of anti-tank guns suddenly appear from behind these houses. Sometimes they got in a round or two before the tank guns blasted them, but it took only one solid hit to kill a Sherman and those anti-tank guns could do it.

Or a *Panzerfaust* squad might unexpectedly start firing their rockets from nearby forest growths. Those things could burn a tank in seconds. There was nothing secure, not even the armor plate between the men in the tank and the troops outside. Of thirty-five tanks in Freeman's batallion, ten had drowned coming in on the beachhead, fifteen had been either burned or blown to hell, and five had pooped out and were abandoned. Five were left and God only knows how that number would be revised before the rest of these hedgerows were finally taken.

Rod Carter put all the horses into high gear and charged straight toward the farmhouse. Freeman kept his eyes glued to the periscope slit. So far it looked okay. Nothing moved; it was just an old farmhouse standing there, innocent victim to what was about to happen to it.

The ground turned soft and muddy. The tank went into second gear, growling its way along, while Freeman tried to observe the farmhouse through the slit. The tank bounced so much it was impossible. Freeman reached up and threw the hatch open. He hauled himself up, just letting his eyes clear the hatch opening. Now he could see. He could also get his head blown off, but there was no other way.

Dandy was waddling along, keeping pace. Her commander trusted more to the periscope and they were buttoned up securely. Freeman never had been a man to like the confines of the tank. He wanted that hatch open as often as possible.

The counterattack came by some prearranged signal, or the Kraut units were wired in to get the word. From either side of the farmhouse, German soldiers rolled out the anti-tank guns. There were a pair of them. At the same moment, the thick brush and woods surrounding the farm, disgorged German soldiers in their field gray uniforms, and some of them were equipped with the *Panzerfausts*.

"Fire!" Freeman yelled.

Mike Amory couldn't possibly have heard him over the roar of the twin engines and the clank of the threads. He didn't have to hear. Mike saw it all through his slit. The 75 flamed. Mike was good with it. The A-P shell burst almost in the face of one anti-tank crew and the gun itself was lifted and thrown aside. At the same time Terry Kiley's machine gun opened up on the foot soldiers and the doughs started work with their M-I's. The advancing line of gray began to slow as it was chopped to pieces, but there were enough of the bazookamen to launch their rockets and those men knew how to shoot.

So did the remaining anti-tank gunner. Freeman saw the flash. *Daisy* was delivered a blow mighty as the crash of a gigantic sledge. It was followed by another hit and the tank staggered and lurched to a stop. The doughs clinging to the back of it were blown off and lay stunned on the ground, while Kraut guns opened up on them.

Suddenly *Dandy* was stopped in its tracks and smoke began to funnel out of the slits. The hatch cover was thrown back. Tony Barone, commander of *Dandy*, started to hoist himself up and out. A Kraut bullet hit him under the jaw. He fell over to one side.

Freeman slid down. "Mike . . . traverse right. Traverse right," he shrieked.

Mike was already traversing the gun to aim at the second anti-tank weapon. The 75 barked again . . . and then again. Mike was shooting well, but his aim was even better now for *Daisy* stood dead in her tracks too and he didn't have to compensate for the lurching and jolting of the tank.

The third H-E hit the anti-tank gun squarely and it disappeared, somehow blown back around the corner of the farmhouse. The heavy stuff was now disposed of, but the price hadn't been light and there were still the bazookamen to worry about.

Daisy was jolted once more. Suddenly the inside of the tank began to feel like the bottom of a fast-heated frying pan. Smoke curled up from grease heated almost to the burning point.

"We're burning," Rod Carter yelled. "Everybody out! We're burning."

Freeman hoisted himself up, cleared the hatch, slid down the side of the tank. He raced across the fifty yards or more toward *Dandy*. Halfway to it, Freeman could see Tony lift his arm in a piteous signal for help. Freeman reached the tank, scrambled onto it and his hand almost touched Tony when the tank blew up.

Whether its gas tank did it, or another *Panzerfaust*, it made little difference. Sergeant Freeman died in the space of a tenth of a second; every man under that armor died and *Dandy* died with them.

Terry Kiley saw it through his bow slit. He screamed as he saw Freeman vanish in that holocaust. Terry saw it all, but never stopped throwing steel. The 75 was kicking too as Sal fed the shells into the hot maw of the cannon and Mike blew up the farmhouses with two well-placed bursts. But it was hopeless. The work of *Daisy* was over too. The heat grew worse.

"Let's get the hell outa here," Carter yelled.

The doughs were taking good care of the Germans, killing them fast and driving the survivors back into the brush. They were no longer helped by the tanks, but the armor had done its work and the doughs raced forward toward the brush, guns spitting.

Terry Kiley fired his last burst from a belt that felt hot and seemed to be smoking. In a minute the ammo would start going off. He clambered out of the bog seat and jumped to the ground. Mike Amory was already there, pressed against the hot side of the tank, not sure which way to run. Sal Monda crawled out, jumped and hightailed it toward the gap in the hedgerow he'd helped to blast.

Rod Carter popped out of the front of the tank and followed Sal. Kiley and Amory picked up their feet and raced after them. They followed the direction of Sal Monda's arm and turned right. They

11

threw themselves down in the mud and dirt behind the hedgerow and all four lay there, panting, bushed, unable to speak, the horror of their brush with death still shining in their eyes.

Monda found his voice first. "Did you see him? Did you see that crazy bastard? He cut across to help Tony, but the goddamn fool musta known he didn't have a chance. *Dandy* was on fire."

"He made it," Carter said. "He made the tank okay and he coulda helped Tony and the rest of them, but the goddamn tank blew up in his face. Nobody can figure on that."

"Well, we lost us a hell of a fine commander," Mike Amory commented and there were tears in his eyes, dampening the grime below them. He rubbed an even dirtier hand across his face and smeared the tear tracings.

"We lost a damn good tank, too," Kiley commented sadly. "Tank and commander, both gone. And after all we went through! Twenty days from D-Day and we get it."

"We're lucky we didn't really get it," Monda said. He had a shrill voice anyway and now it was an excited squeak. After a while the high notes would give way to his normal tenor voice, but right now he sounded like an excited housewife over a back fence when she heard the high-school girl next door was pregnant.

Amory was a tall man from Arkansas, but lean as a hungry Texan. He rolled over on his back and stared at the sky and wondered what they thought up there about all this bloodshed and fire and destruction.

Rod Carter was the heaviest of the four. A New Englander, he didn't speak too much, but they'd quickly learned that he meant what he said. Back at camp in England, Sal Monda hadn't believed this at first, but he found out after he got knocked on his tail and a quietly seething Rod Carter stood over him waiting for him to get up. Instead, Sal had merely rasied his hand to be helped to his feet in a gesture of both surrender and forgiveness. Rod had hauled him up and patted him on the back and nobody ever mentioned the incident again. Sal couldn't even remember how it had started. He was sure Rod remembered, but if he did, he never brought it up.

Kiley was a medium-sized man, just right for the bog seat and he was a fine machine gunner. Usually he didn't have to think of what to say. He talked for the sake of talking, but now he was silent. There were things he didn't want to talk about—like what he'd seen happen to Sergeant Freeman.

Rod Carter suddenly rolled over half a dozen times, splashing into the mud at the base of the gap in the hedgerow. He wiped mud from his eyes and looked out over the cleared space. *Dandy* was burning fiercely, but *Daisy* stood there with only a little curl of smoke coming from its hatch.

"Hey," he called out, "that goddamn tin can ain't on fire. Hell, we hauled ass too soon."

"We hauled hot asses," Sal shouted back. "It was time to leave when we did."

"Yeah . . . yeah . . ." Carter studied the tank, "but she ain't burning now. She looks okay. Real okay."

"Wanta go pat her on the tits?" Amory shouted.

"What tits?" Sal asked.

13

"Her name's *Daisy*, ain't it?" Amory asked.

"Too much small-arms stuff flying around." Carter rolled back to his former position. "I think *Daisy* got herself drilled through. I'm not sure, but one of them bursts felt like something busted."

"An 88 caromed off her left side," Kiley explained. "I saw it through my gun slit. That's what stopped us. The first one was a head-on burst that the sandbags took, but the second was a sideswipe and about the same time one of them goddamn Panzerfaust rockets smacked us on the same side, about in the same place and that was it. But the *Panzerfaust* didn't start us burning. It must have been defective because it didn't burn until it was on the ground."

"You mean it roasted the tank even from the ground?" Sal asked in awe. "Hell's bells, I don't wanna be around when one of them things makes a direct hit."

"Get your balls fried off," Carter commented. "Look, who's in command now? What're we gonna do? We got no leader. We got no tank. We got nothin'."

"Wait'll I take a look," Kiley said. He started rolling toward the gap. Standing up could be dangerous. Usually snipers were left in the hedgerows and those who didn't surrender, died killing Americans.

Kiley didn't delay long. He rolled back, wiped caked mud from his face and spat noisily to get the stuff out of his mouth.

"Like Rod said, *Daisy* looks okay. What say we go back and see if we can get her started."

"Hell," Carter said, "she died on me. Besides, the gas

14

tank may still be hot and dangerous. You saw what happened to *Dandy*."

"We can find out," Kiley said. "At least see if she'll run, for Gawd's sake."

"Lemme go," Carter said. "When it comes to starting her, she's my baby."

"Hell, let's all go," Kiley said. "Come on . . . if there are snipers left, we'll have to risk 'em. The doughs cleaned out the hedges pretty good. We just gotta find out if *Daisy's* dead."

Carter arose this time, looked about anxiously, ran to the gap, stopped and waited. Nothing happened. No whine of a sniper's slug preceded the smack of a bullet. Carter cleared the gap and ran straight toward the tank.

Kiley waited until Carter reached the stalled metal monster and then he cut for it. By that time Amory and Monda figured if Kiley and Carter drew no fire, it was safe enough. They trotted unconcernedly toward the tank.

As they reached it, Carter started looking it over. They could hear him grunting, but whether it was in anguish at what he saw or in plain bewilderment, they weren't able to tell. He reached the front of the tank.

"I'm gonna go in," he said. "Better wait until I see how hot she is. Outside, she cooled off okay."

Monda placed the flat of his hand against the side of the tank. The metal was more than normally warm, but it wasn't the heat that precedes or follows a tank fire. There's no mistaking that temperature.

Carter settled himself in the driver's seat. The switch

15

was still on. He couldn't see any real damage. There'd been a deep dent in her side, but otherwise she wasn't hurt so far as he could tell.

He was sure her engines had conked out and he felt even surer when he trod on the starter and got only a loud whine. He tried again with the same result.

"How about it?" Monda called from somewhere out front.

"I dunno—sounds dead, but you never can tell. She always was a reluctant son of a bitch."

He used the starter again. This time the engine sputtered a little and Carter's hopes began to rise. On the sixth try the Wright engines caught and the tank was filled with the smell of high octane. They turned over and they caught and they purred. Outside, somebody gave a yell. Carter heard them scrambling aboard. He backed away slowly, testing her, waiting for the tread to slip or something else to give, but *Daisy* didn't die easily. She might be pocked, blackened, dented and mud-spattered, but she moved. She wasn't any beauty-parade winner, but she moved like a big-breasted, fat-assed concierge Carter had kidded in a French café two days ago. Both had the stately roll and grace of an elephant.

Carter turned her just before they reached the gap and he rolled her slowly toward the rear. Nobody knew what would happen now. Nobody knew how many of the original battalion survived. Certainly no more than four with *Dandy* now gone, but they had to find out. They had to be reassigned and given a new commander.

Everyone knew that whoever he turned out to be, he'd never match Freeman for courage, or patience or a blistering tongue when things went wrong. They were used to it, losing someone. They'd seen it happen too often, but they were still affected. They still knew how to grieve, though it might not be with tears, except for that one brief moment when Carter had given way.

TWO

DAISY HAD BEEN scrubbed free of mud, greased, polished and an ammo carrier had deposited a hundred and fifty 75's at her side. Their brass shells gleamed softly in the morning sunlight that filtered through the apple trees of the orchard where *Daisy* was in bivouac. Boxes of machine gun ammo were stacked up and *Daisy* had all the high octane she could hold. They were ready for action but no word came through. The whole battalion had settled down for what had been a week of rest and idleness.

Carter was shaving with the hot water he'd heated in his helmet. Amory was stretched out under a tree, his back against the truck and he slept with his mouth wide open. Sal Monda had the gas burner going and was busy with four eggs he'd scrounged from a farmer, turning them into the damnedest omelet mess Kiley had ever seen.

"Jeeze, Sal, can't you even fry an egg without mussing it all up like that?"

"My eggs." Sal was unabashed. "Happens I like 'em this way. You're just jealous. Hell, I'll bet I can bake a better cake than you."

"Not if there's eggs in it."

Sal forgot the congealing white and yellow mess in the pan. He was looking straight ahead, at the soldier who approached them.

"You see what I see?"

"Speakin' of eggs," Kiley squinted in the newcomer's direction, "this looks like a tough one."

Carter paused in the middle of a razor stroke down his cheek and looked. The soldier was a sergeant, which didn't surprise them because they'd been expecting one. But the man himself did. He was short, stocky, with a powerful build and a fat neck creased in sun-reddened layers. He was bandy-legged and he walked with a rolling gait like a sailor too long at sea. He wasn't wearing his helmet. In dangled from his belt, a BAR slung over one shoulder. Except for a light fringe of hair, he was bald. As he drew nearer, they could see that his eyes were a cold blue, but clear. Not the eyes of a heavy drinker or a man who'd rather hell around than sleep.

He swung the musette bag off his shoulder and dropped it on the ground.

"I'm Dixon. Bert Dixon. I'm replacing your commander."

"Hi," Sal said non-committally. He never went

18

over-board for any superior until he had the full measure of the man.

"I'm Terry Kiley, Sergeant." Kiley held out his hand. "My pal here is Sal Monda. I ride bog, he's loader. The guy shaving is Rod Carter, our driver, and the sleeping beauty under the tree is Mike Amory, gunner."

"Hey, Sarge," Sal stirred the eggs, "as one friend to another, ain't you kinda old for a tanker?"

"Like to take me on?"

"Hell, I never meant that, but this is kinda rugged . . ."

Sergeant Dixon placed his BAR on top of the musette bag. "How long you been a tanker, son?"

"Well . . . right from the start . . . I trained in England . . ."

"Right from the start? You know where tanks started? In France—in 1917. I rode a French-made tank against the Germans then. French-made and loaned to us because we didn't have a goddamn stinking tank to our name. But we got 'em and they were a hell of a lot better'n that frog hunk of junk. And we kept getting 'em and from that day to this I never been outa the tanks. Now what were you saying about something being rugged?"

"You . . . were in World War One?" Kiley marveled.

"I was eighteen. I was a doughfoot through Saint-Mihiel with the Big Red One. When the Division came out of reserve again, I was in a tank and we rode into the Argonne Forest and didn't come out again for eleven days."

"In a forest? With a tank?" Sal asked in a stunned voice.

"When we broke out of there, the Huns . . . that's what we called them in those days . . . started running and we went after them. We didn't stop until we were thrown into reserve again before the next push."

"No kiddin', Sarge," Kiley said. "How would the old tanks stand up against a Sherman?"

Against the weapons we got now, they were cheese boxes, but in them days tanks were new and there weren't any anti-tank guns or bazookas, so we didn't do too bad."

Rod Carter finished his shaving chore, but didn't wash his face yet. Sal found the eggs scorched, but he ate them anyway, out of the pan. Kiley lit a butt and rapidly got the idea that this rooster of a man who would replace Freeman was good.

"You been army all your life?" he asked.

"I married the friggin' army," Dixon said. "We been a happy pair. That's a crummy looking tank you got."

"It's a veteran," Sal said. "We rolled onto the beach on D-Day and we ain't stopped since."

"You got any hot-line stuff about when we move out, Sarge?" Kiley asked.

"I will have sometime today. I'm due at a CP Briefing in twenty minutes. All I know right now is we got a new Colonel."

"What happened to Colonel Catlin?" Sal wanted to know, referring to the present battalion commander.

"I don't know. This is some kind of a new operation under a new man. I don't even know who he is."

"Goddamn," Carter commented sourly. "I kinda

figured we might be sent back to Merry England to train some new cadres. You mean we're gonna move into more action, Sarge?"

"You wanta earn your keep, don't you? Somebody take care of my BAR and my bag. I'll be back pretty soon and maybe I'll have the word."

Dixon walked over to where Amory was still asleep. He prodded him lightly in the ribs. "Remember me to this guy," he said.

They watched him walk away, bandy legs moving as if he were on parade. Amory was rubbing his eyes.

"What's happened? Who the hell kicked me?"

Kiley motioned toward the retreating back of the sergeant. "Meet Dixon, new tank commander. He was a tanker in World War One."

"Jesus, he must be older'n my old man," Amory said. "He didn't even make World War One."

"This guy did and he don't mind letting you know about it," Kiley commented.

"I kinda had an idea something was up," Sal grumbled, "when they dumped a hundred and fifty rounds. We usually carry a hundred rounds of that stuff and if we gotta cram in fifty more, somebody's gonna get a round ass sittin' on top of it."

"Let's get 'em stowed," Kiley suggested. "Nothing like polishing the apple for the new sarge."

"Yeah, especially since he looks like he could polish all of us off, three at a time," Sal said. He scraped the rest of the egg out of the pan, unconcernedly used the still-hot water in Carter's helmet to rinse the pan. He dried it with a bunch of grass, harvested from the foot of the tree and carried it over to the tank. He tossed it through the hatch and listened to its rattle its way down.

So far, Mike Amory hadn't moved. He was still propped against the tree trunk, a little sore because he'd been awakened from a dream inspired by the letter from Julie which he'd read just before he fell asleep.

She'd written how she'd been making plans for their new house. Some bill had just gone through Congress giving a GI certain privileges in getting a new home and she was going to take advantage of it. Amory only vaguely knew what she was talking about, but she was a practical soul, this red-headed, winsome Julie whom he loved and if she said it was so, that's how it was. A house would be nice to move into right after they got back from their honeymoon.

He had written her every day this last week in bivouac and he'd received two letters from her, another from his mother and a letter addressed to him, but meant for the group, from Sergeant Freeman's father.

They'd written a round-robin letter telling him how Bill had left the security of his tank to cross a fire zone and reach a sister tank where the commander had been hurt and was hanging out of the hatch. How he'd climbed onto the tank and was getting the wounded man loose when the whole thing blew up. They made it clear Bill hadn't suffered, hadn't felt a thing, likely. They'd written about him as their pal, and made a point of emphasizing he was their superior, but they never regarded him as such.

It hadn't been an easy letter to write, but it had been from the heart and apparently Bill's father recognized this. His answer was chatty, full of thanks that his son had met a crew like this. It had made them all feel better.

To Amory, here weren't many breaks in action for a tanker, but during every one the war seemed to recede and stand off far away. Where he didn't have to worry about a rumbling sound of enemy armor, or a scream of sound in the air as a *Stuka* dived, or whistling bullets and whining shells. Away from the front, the war simply ceased to exist for him. He possessed the faculty for dropping it from his mind, except for the routine duties required of a tanker reprieved to a short rest.

He'd gone into the tank corps automatically. He didn't ask for it. He didn't have to—he'd been a foreman mechanic in a big Detroit auto plant. A foreman at twenty because he knew how to make an engine talk and when he met the twin Wright airplane engines used in a Sherman medium, he fell in love with them. This was his element in war. Here he was good. Meant for the kind of fighting a tanker had to do. As a doughfoot he'd have slogged unhappily wherever he was ordered, but in tanks he was at home.

Take *Daisy* now. She was beat up, nearly holed; she had more scars than a punch-drunk fighter on a barn circuit. But her armor was intact, her engines were sweet, her guns were accurate and she had the crew who knew how to handle her. His job was to use the 75 and kill Germans with it. The more he killed, the sooner he'd go home.

If there had to be a war, this was Mike Amory's kind. He closed his eyes again, trying to bring back the dream of the house Julie had described. It wouldn't return. While Amory had not heard Dixon give the word, he sensed that they were going to move out soon. He decided to write another letter.

Every one he wrote could be his last. He was sensibly aware of that fact. He had to tell Julie how he felt about that house in case anything happened. There was a USO setup near CP. He walked slowly in that direction. He'd find V-mail paper and they'd post it for him. He was planning the letter as he walked, intending it to be carefree. He'd write about the new sergeant, so capable he'd been a tanker since the days of the first armor. Julie would find some comfort in that. Mike Amory didn't, but he knew Julie would.

The others, Sal Monda, Kiley and Carter were packing up. This had been a nice camp and they hated to leave it, but maybe there'd be others. There was always that hope they might liberate Paris and bivouac there for a few weeks.

That, Sal Monda thought, would be the millennium for a soldier. French broads were going to be very grateful when the Krauts were chased out of Paris. Sal didn't think he'd mind getting some of their gratitude, for he'd heard it was on a most practical basis. There were good points to war sometimes. At home he'd been considered too much a kid to play it heavy with any of the local girls. They wanted older men and all left to him were the high school sophomores. But a French dame . . . . now that would be something not to write home about. He rubbed his stubble of beard, but decided he wouldn't get to Paris for some time yet and to hell with shaving.

Terry Kiley yelled for Sal to get aboard and stack

the ammo. While he passed it, he wondered where they'd go next. There had been some rumor—very official, according to the men who came up with it— that they were going to start a big push with General Patton's armor. He was a rough guy, but he got things done. Kiley thought he'd like to serve under him, because that was one way to help shorten the war. It couldn't end too soon for him.

He had an education in teaching to finish and snatching years out of his youth could set him too far back. He looked ahead to some small ivy-covered college in a small town where he could settle down, find some nice girl, get married, raise a family and build the tradition of the school. His ambitions went that far and no further, which he believed was exactly right.

Rod Carter, standing on the tank, taking the ammo from Kiley and handing it down to Sal inside the tank, wasn't thinking about home. He didn't have any. Being a soldier, a tanker, was fine with him. There was food, excitement, a little money for a bottle and a woman when he wanted one and he was located where he could find one. Nobody at home he cared a damn about. He wouldn't ever go back. He was glad Sergeant Dixon had taken over the command. Dixon said he'd married the army. Carter had thought about it and now he could get some expert advice on the subject.

The ammo was stowed. Sal's large metal storage box he'd scrounged from an officer's barracks in England was crammed with food and lashed down. The Coleman stove for heating was fueled and packed along with the old battered coffee pot and the fry pan.

A jeep rolled up and grease-coated BAR's were un-loaded in their original boxes, along with ammo for them. There was a crate of grenades. The *Daisy* crew stood around and looked at the loot.

"What the hell are they gonna do with us?" Kiley asked. "All that gear!"

"Be glad you ain't a doughfoot." Sal found some solace in being a tanker. "Grenades, yet! And have a look at the boxes of rations. We're traveling heavy, pals, and it looks like we're going far. I wonder where the hell it'll turn out to be."

Amory peered around. "The other tanks didn't get this stuff. It was routed straight to us and nobody else. Maybe we're gonna fight a one-tank war."

"And maybe our new Sergeant wouldn't like that," Carter commented. "Not that I don't think he can't do it."

"Hey, you think we're being fueled and rested this way so we can start some kind of a long campaign?" Sal asked.

"We got fifty percent more ammo, the engines been serviced, and we been issued BAR's and grenades. We sure ain't heading back to some rest camp," Amory said.

Sal scrambled out of the turret and jumped to the ground. He caught up his helmet, jammed it on his head. "I'll be back. Just in case we get hung up some place, I wanna get me wine, bread and cheese. And some more eggs. Eggs are important to a guy. They make a balanced diet. Give you staying power and we might wind up in Paris. See you guys around."

As Sal scampered off, Kiley rubbed his jaw. "That

guy may have something. I'm going to lay in a supply of cigarettes and a little whiskey if I can get it."

"Get me some plug," Carter begged. "Plenty of it. When I get this baby carriage rolling over rough ground, I just shove a hunk of plug between my teeth and they chew it automatically. The bumps do it. And a bottle of brandy, huh?"

He handed Kiley a ten dollar bill and then Carter picked up one of the BAR's and began to clean it. He liked guns. The feel of a BAR was comforting, like the skin of a woman. Hot in love and combat.

He was completely engrossed in the workings of the gun when a shadow fell across his stretched-out legs. He looked up. Sergeant Dixon was surveying the tank.

"Where's everybody?" he asked.

"Off . . . here and there, Sarge."

"Find 'em. Alert 'em. We're pulling out soon. I mean damn soon."

Kiley scrambled to his feet and laid the gun down carefully. "Where we moving to, Sarge? You got any news?"

"Yeah, I know where we're going, but you don't and you won't until we get under way. It's top-secret stuff . . . big stuff."

"Action, huh?"

"Pal," Dixon said, "you'll see so much action you won't think you been in a war until now. You got two hours. Write a letter home if you want to. There won't be another chance for maybe two months."

"Jesus, where we going? Russia?"

"And don't forget the pineapples." Dixon kicked the crate of grenades. "Oh yeah . . . I'll tell you the assembly point when we pull outa here. Everybody in battle jackets. Sweaters under them—and side arms. Where they're supposed to be and not worn like a Texan cowboy gun. Be sure to alert the others. If we're late, there'll be hell to pay."

THREE

THE CORPORAL in Major General Stratton's outer office was accustomed to dealing with brass and he willingly stood up to salute only when two or more stars passed his desk.

The jeep roared up and stopped so noisily that the Corporal raised his head and glanced out the window beside the desk. He watched the tall, somewhat heavily-set man with iron gray hair under his garrison cap, get out of the jeep and stand a moment as if getting his bearings. The sunlight reflected against his face and lighted the icy blueness of his eyes. He wasn't a handsome man by any stretch of the imagination, but there seemed to be a measured firmness in this man, as definite as in his long strides toward the door.

The Corporal came to his feet before the Colonel entered and he tossed off a snappy salute which the Colonel returned with precision.

"I'm Colonel Hagen. The General's expecting me."

"Yes sir, Colonel Hagen, he sure is. Been gettin' a little impatient too. Right this way, sir."

The Corporal opened the door for the Colonel and Hagen stepped into the office. General Stratton looked up, got to his feet and quickly walked around the desk to shake hands with the Colonel.

"Luke," he said, "it's good to see you again. Been at least five years."

"Yes sir, at least," Colonel Hagen acknowledged. "What have you been doing?"

"Up to now, I've been holding down a desk in the States. I take it you're responsible for my being here on thirty hours notice."

"Did you mind, Luke? Sit down, man. The new star on my shoulder doesn't mean a thing to us. Frankly, you rated it more than I. How have you been?"

"Fine, now that I'm assigned here."

General Stratton returned to his desk and settled himself in the chair. "I asked for you, Luke, because I don't know of any buzz saw quite like you. And for this operation a buzz saw is what we need. It's a bitchy job, but right down your alley. I predict you'll eat it up. However, one hitch. I asked for a star for you. The operation rates it. They said no."

"I understand. Thanks anyway, Frank. It used to hurt like hell. I've grown accustomed to it or I've grown a thick hide. At any rate, forget it."

"It's a stinking shame no matter how you look at it. Things that happened so long ago . . . well . . . ."

"I'd rather not discuss it, Frank, if you don't mind. Sometimes memories have a razor edge."

29

"All right, Luke. Just this one further thing. I've all the faith in the world in you."

"Thanks again."

"As you know, we've got the Germans pretty much on the run. Patton's rocked 'em off balance. Monty's sitting on his tail as usual, but he's building up a big force—at our expense, I might add . . . but the size of his operation looks tremendous to the Germans. I can't say when he'll get it off the ground. There's our main trouble. While we wait for him, Patton gets stalled by lack of fuel and ammo to say nothing of a lack of men. While Patton has to cool his heels, the Germans are regrouping, and bringing men to stand in Patton's way. Now we have in mind a small operation, as tank operations go, but one hell of an important one."

"A limited breakthrough," Colonel Luke Hagen said. "I've advocated the use of a strike force during all the time I trained men how to fight with tanks. It had to be that when you asked for me."

"All right, that's the deal exactly. We've picked thirty-five tanks, all in reasonably good shape, with the best crews available. We intend to fake an attack all along the line with massive artillery barrages, a big air strike, plenty of movement of troops and a widespread operation with tank forces. Under cover of all this noise and confusion, your thirty-five tanks will penetrate the German lines. After that, it's up to you, but that shouldn't be any problem because you wrote the book on this sort of operation."

"What about supplies and replacements?"

"You'll carry a communications truck. Use this and we'll set up rendezvous points where you can refuel and rest. You'll operate clandestinely—hit-and-run stuff. Sometimes there'll be specific assignments; other times you blast anything worth hitting. The idea is to keep them jittery. Never let them know how small your force is—or how big, for that matter. Keep 'em guessing. Don't give them time to regroup or strengthen their lines. In other words, drive 'em crazy."

"When do we put this into operation?"

"Tomorrow. You'll move out tonight, get your tanks set for the quick drive under our diversions. I've arranged for all tank commanders in your unit to meet you in a briefing room. That'll be the barn—but we've got it wired for electricity. There's even a canteen. All the latest inventions and comforts."

Colonel Hagen looked around the large room. "You've done very well for yourself, sir. Farmhouse, of course?"

"Knock on the walls." General Stratton invited with a grin. "More than plaster and lathe. The Germans used it as a CP and those walls are two feet of cement."

"Not bad. Better than the CP's we had in the States. Remember that rat-infested lean-to in the Philippines?"

"I remember. Wonder how things are there now, with the Japs in control. Poor devils who were taken at Corregidor."

"Last I heard, we're fighting back, sir. The marines are storming islands, chain-hopping to Tokyo. I asked to be sent there. They didn't even answer my request."

"You're still bitter, Luke. After all these years. Oh, I don't blame you. I'd have probably done something more drastic than you did, but this old hatred is bad for a man."

"It's more resignation than hatred," the Colonel said. "Years make a difference, but there are memories, Frank. They hurt like hell. That's why I'm so damned grateful to you for getting me this assignment. I'm a fighting man, not a pencil pusher. I've been slowly going crazy."

"When you get back from this private war you're starting tomorrow, we'll talk about it and see what's to be done in getting you the star or stars you richly deserve."

Colonel Hagen shook his head and allowed himself a small smile. "I'm not bucking for it, Frank. I'm fifty years old. I'm a retread."

"You're as trim as a buck private after his thirteen week induction period. I outweigh you, but I'd hate to tackle you, even with help." He consulted his watch. "Time to start the briefing. Major Jenkins will read you the maps, detail the jump-off, get you set up. Relay this to your tank commanders. Major Ballard will be your aide. We've already selected the other officers, but most important will be your tank commanders. Get along with them and you win wars."

"They're liable to look on me as an old fogy who never got beyond Colonel because he's too dumb."

Major General Stratton threw back his head and laughed out loud. "I'd like to be there if anybody ever said that to your face. Wish there was time to have you for dinner. We liberated a very fine French chef. I'm beginning to run to fat. Well—get on with it."

Hagen stood up. "Yes, sir. Thanks again, Frank."

"You're doing me the favor, Luke, remember that.

There's just nobody else who can handle this the way I know you will."

Outside, the corporal stood up again and showed the Colonel to Major Jenkin's office. It was upstairs, in what used to be a small bedroom. There were maps nailed to all the walls and a large map-reading table in the middle of the floor.

Jenkins was one of the best. He could read things from maps Hagen would have missed and never known it. For an hour he and Jenkins bent over the maps and Hagen made notes. He was given a leather-bound set and other sets were to be distributed to each commander just before they took off.

Hagen didn't look up Major Ballard, who'd be his aide. He went straight to the barn where thirty-five tank commanders, mostly sergeants with a sprinkling of second lieutenants, were waiting. Ballard was there. Hagen recognized him at once for the type that got things done. Perhaps annoying in the way he did it, but efficient and helpful. A medium-sized man of about 30 with a ready grin. Hagen liked him.

"Attention!" A sergeant called sharply.

The audience stood up quickly. Colonel Hagen walked to the small platform which sagged as if it might buckle under him.

"I'm Colonel Hagen," he introduced himself. "You men will command specially selected tanks and crews for a very special job which should prove to be a lot of fun."

"I don't like the way he says fun," one of the sergeants whispered to his neighbor.

"Who the hell is he?" another asked.

"He's from the States," Sergeant Dixon said softly. "He's been in tanks almost as long as I have."

"Is he any good?"

"He's the best tanker in the business. Personally, he's a miserable bastard."

"Boy, you do know him, don't you?"

"I know him," Dixon said in a cold voice.

Hagen called for the large maps, set them up and began to point out the territory they would work through.

"We're a strike force," he explained, "with no special objectives unless they come through specifically. Our job is to harass and kill. We hit, run like hell, hide and hit again. You might say we'll act like old western outlaw bands in the movies, but this will be for real. We'll be constantly surrounded by the enemy and if we're caught, we'll very likely be shot. This will be no picnic. Combat rarely is, but we'll see action and we'll do our part to shorten this war. Maps will be issued; our techniques will be instituted after we crash through. We move out in two hours, rendezvous at dawn, wait for hell to break loose and sneak in under cover of it. Any questions?"

"You riding a tank, sir?" a lieutenant asked.

"No, Lieutenant, I'll ride a jeep. That'll be my command car. Supplies and replacements will reach us as we need them. We're in for a rugged time and I can't even tell you how long it will last, but our work is of the utmost importance. I want every man to know that. Any more questions?"

"How far toward Berlin will we make it?" a sergeant asked. There was no note of facetiousness in his voice.

"I don't know, Sergeant. We play this entirely by ear. Our greatest problem will be to hide. They'll send everything at us, once they know we're loose. We may have to split up in small groups or even proceed singly. One thing I can tell you. I've advocated a force of this kind for years. If they'd let me test it during peacetime maneuvers, we might be more efficient, but we're going to make it all the way. Tell your men to trust me."

"Trust him, he says," Sergeant Dixon muttered.

"Huh? What'd you say, Sarge?"

"I was talking to myself."

"Think he's as good as he says he is?"

"Better."

"But a bastard too, huh?"

"Yes. . . ."

"What'd he ever do to you, Sarge?"

Dixon eyed the younger man at his side. "Nothing," he said curtly. "To me he didn't do a damn thing."

They were dismissed and Dixon made his way back to his tank. The men had her loaded and ready, he was glad to see. There were new sandbags wired to her blunt nose, and her name had been painted out along with her number. These boys knew their business, Dixon decided. He called them together and he leaned against the tank as he spoke.

"We move out in less than two hours, rendezvous and wait for morning. That's when you'll find out where we're going and why. Leave all personal possessions behind, take off your shoulder patches, don't carry letters or pictures. Before we take off, I'm going to inspect those BAR's and your side arms. I want them clean and I want your knives sharp. That's all."

35

Dixon slung his musette bag onto the tank and started climbing after it. A motorcycle sidecar pulled up.

"Sergeant Dixon here?" the driver asked.

"Yeah . . . I'm Dixon."

"Get in the bathtub," the driver ordered. "Colonel wants to see you."

"What Colonel?"

"Hagen. And right now, pal."

Dixon fitted his bulk into the sidecar. It made a sharp U-turn and roared back.

Carter said, "You ever see an expression like that? You'd think the name Hagen was a slap in the puss."

"Wonder what's between them?" Sal mused. "Something sure is."

"It's none of our business if you ask me," Kiley said.

"Hey—did they ever ask for volunteers for this mission?"

"Don't be a horse's ass. Who'd go?" Sal asked.

"They're supposed to ask for volunteers if the mission is dangerous," Kiley persisted.

"What's dangerous about it?" Amory asked. "All we've got to do is shoot up the whole Kraut army, win the war and go home."

"We don't even know where we're going." Sal complained. "It must be a suicide job. Who thinks up these things, anyway?"

"I dunno, Sal," Kiley replied, "but I'll take bets whoever he is, he's nice and safe in some cozy office and he shacks up every night and lives on champagne and steak."

Mike Amory said, "Let's cut out this crap and make sure we're set."

Sergeant Dixon found Colonel Hagen seated in a jeep, pulled up some distance from CP. Dixon climbed out of the motorcycle, came to attention and saluted smartly while the messenger roared away on his noisy machine.

Hagen touched the peak of his helmet casually. "Get aboard, Sergeant. I want to talk to you."

"I'd rather stand here, sir. I'm comfortable on my feet, if you don't mind, sir."

Hagen's face clouded. "Still feel that way, eh? All right. I had an idea you would. That's why I sent for you. I didn't know you were in this group until I saw you. Putting aside any personal differences, I regard you as one of the best non-commissioned men in the army. We're going on a dangerous job, Bert. There's no room for hatred on a mission like this. I don't give one single damn how you feel about me, but you'll take my orders and you'll handle them like any soldier would. If you cross me up, I'll send you back. Do you understand?"

"Yes sir. Don't worry about it, sir. I know what I'm supposed to do."

"I'm sure of it, but if you feel your dislike for me is so great that you won't be able to take my orders and carry them out to the letter, you're to remain here. Clear?"

"Yes sir."

"You'll come with us then?"

"Yes sir."

"All right. Dismissed."

Dixon saluted again, turned precisely, started away.

"Bert," the Colonel called.

Dixon kept moving.

"Dixon!" Hagen said sharply.

The sergeant came to a prompt halt, wheeled and stood there, his face a blank.

"When I call you, stop!"

"When you call me Sergeant, or Dixon, I'll stop, sir. When you call me Bert, I don't hear you."

"You're a damned, stubborn idiot."

"Yes, sir. What did the Colonel wish, sir?"

"I . . . the hell with it. Nothing! Drag your ass, Sergeant."

Dixon allowed a very faint smile to cross his lips. He pivoted and walked briskly away. Colonel Hagen lit a cigarette, smoked it half through and flung it away. He was going to be glad to get into action. When death lurked close by, there was no time for thinking and all he'd done for twelve years now, was think. Think and think and think and never come to an answer.

In a few hours he'd lead a hundred and seventy-five fighting men into battle. One of them possessed enough hatred to shoot him in the back. He was tempted to order Dixon to leave the battalion, but that would only have been an indication of his own weakness.

Colonel Luke Hagen didn't intend to give Sergeant Bert Dixon one damned thing to gloat about. Not now or ever.

FOUR

STRIKE FORCE, code name Javelin, crossed over into German held territory at 0600, after one hour of steady bombardment by artillery, bombings by three hundred P-47 fighter-bombers and fifty Flying Forts. Tanks, not attached to Javelin, moved out with their guns hammering and infantry launched what they actually believed to be a genuine all-out frontal assault.

Colonel Hagen picked up his radio in the jeep. "Dingo Command to all tank commanders. On the release of smoke, move out in single file formation. We'll proceed twenty-six miles at a steady speed of thirty-five miles an hour. By the time we reach our point, the fake attack will be over and we'd better be hidden. All commanders acknowledge and when you sign off, no more radio contact under any circumstances. Report!"

Dixon spoke into his mike. "Dingo Commander One. Ready to move out."

One by one the other tank commanders, in order, reported in, using the special code call. Dixon looked back at the line of tanks, all engines idling. He waited for the signal from the Command Car, a jeep. Colonel Hagen and Major Ballard were twisted around in their seats. As Dixon might have expected, the Colonel was driving his own car. He saw the Colonel's hand raise and then signal forward.

Dixon slid down, pulled the hatch closed after him. "Move out," he ordered and clamped his face to the periscope.

The tank took the lead, as it had been ordered to do. The jeep was rolling slowly, waiting for the smoke. It came in the form of an artillery barrage and co-ordinated with it, another air strike began to blow up everything on both sides of the route the strike force would take.

The jeep picked up some speed and Dixon called for an equal amount, although Rod Carter at the wheel, could observe through his own slit how fast the jeep was traveling. The tanks began to rumble into high gear. They were boldly using a road, hoping they wouldn't leave tracks that way. Hiding thirty-five tanks from the Germans was going to be a problem that would require as much luck as skill.

Ten minutes later they were rolling at thirty-five miles an hour and the sound of the fake attack was growing dim behind them. They had started promptly on schedule and at 0605 they were riding out of the smoke and straight into danger.

Dixon raised the hatch and hauled himself up. He tightened the chin strap of his helmet and breathed in some fresh air. Kiley opened his hatch too and so did Rod Carter. Air circulated through the tank.

Nobody said anything. They were all too well aware of the fact that now there were Germans ahead of them, behind them and on both sides of them. No matter which way they chose, they'd have to fight their way clear.

To Dixon, the prospects looked none too rosy, though he never for a moment discounted Colonel Hagen's ability to bring them out of this. No man, anywhere, knew more than Hagen did about this type of tank warfare.

The road remained good; they saw no signs of German patrols or scouts. No cars or motorcycles passed them and so far as Dixon could see, no enemy planes were in the sky.

Everything the Germans had was probably at the point where they expected a breakthrough. They were probably congratulating themselves by now for being so tough they'd stalled an advance before it really got started.

The countryside was farm land, some of it green and well tended. Most, however, lay fallow, going to weeds and shrubs. Perhaps the bucolic atmosphere even penetrated the tanks, for suddenly Dixon and his crew felt relaxed and the tenseness drained out of them readily.

Strung out behind him were the other tanks, evenly spaced, maintaining the same rate of speed. Thirty-five twin engines must be making an ear-shattering racket, Dixon thought, and how the Germans didn't hear them was a mystery—unless there were no Krauts here—and Hagen would have checked that.

Every mile increased their danger, made the trip back all the harder and more deadly. Dixon surveyed the countryside, now and then sweeping the horizon with his glasses. There was no evidence of any living being. Not even a glimpse of a small town, but that was not surprising because the route would have been carefully selected and the Colonel would have made doubly sure it was the safest.

It was time to tell the crew what to expect. So far they'd gone into this blind and they were entitled to know the truth. Dixon slid down, closed the hatch and picked up the mike connecting him with the crew.

"Okay," he said, "here it is. We're a strike force known as Javelin. We're going through Kraut territory right now and getting deeper and deeper into it every mile we travel. Pretty soon we'll arrive at a place picked out by patrols beforehand, where we can run these tanks under some sort of cover. Our object is to kill Krauts and destroy their property. The general idea is to raise so much hell they'll use a great deal of their equipment trying to find us. There's a hitch in the general advance and they don't want the Krauts to dig in. Any questions?"

"Carter—driver."

"Over to you, Carter."

"What happens if we run across a Kraut tank column? Over."

"We fight. Any more bright questions?" He listened a second or two. "Over and out."

He hauled himself out of the turret again. This time he removed his helmet. It was against regulations, but Dixon never did believe they applied to a career sergeant. He brushed a hand over his bald head. The sun felt good on it. He discovered he was sweating, although the June air was definitely cool. This was almost like mock warfare and, thinking of it, his mind went back to the good years. He thought of Lois, so slim and blonde, so beautiful and full of life and vitality. It had been a long time since he'd thought of her. Somewhere in the African campaign she got lost in his memory, but it required only a few days of peace and quiet to bring her back.

Not for long ... he forced her out of his mind by deliberately making plans for the details of this operation. No girl, real or in memory, had a place there.

He caught the signal from Major Ballard and raised his arm high to send the order along. Speeds were reduced, the jeep made a slow turn down what seemed to be a one-lane country road that led directly into a dense forest. Something like a lumber road in Canada, Dixon thought. Just wide enough so the tanks didn't rip everything down as they rolled along.

The jeep slowed more and then stopped. The line of tanks were now safely along this lane and hidden from the road they'd traveled over. Major Ballard was walking back. The two lieutenants jumped down and hurried forward. Dixon jointed them, but the other tank commanders stayed put.

Major Ballard said, "Sergeant, detail enough men to wipe out the tracks leaving the highway and far enough down this lane so they can't be seen."

"Yes sir," Dixon said. He didn't move. There'd be more orders.

"Mark the spot where the jeep stands now. That will be the location of the last tank. The others will move on, spacing themselves fifty feet apart. As soon as your position is established, break out your camouflage and get it into place at once. There will be no fires, no smoking, no undue noise. You sleep in your tanks if we remain long enough for that. If you have to go to the toilet, move back at least a quarter mile from the lane. Remember this—we're on enemy soil; we're surrounded at all times. There's no easy way back and none at all if the Germans are alerted to our hiding place. That's all."

Dixon ran back to his tank. "Move out until the jeep stops, then stop fifty feet from it and cut your engines. No smoking, no loud talking, no fires. When you go to the can, take a walk first, at least a quarter of a mile."

He waved the tank on as the jeep began to move. The whole line rolled on past Dixon and he waited until the last tank was in position and the last engine cut.

From the communications truck, signal men ran a wire along the whole line of tanks and issued field telephones to each one. No radios could be used, but the field phones were much better anyway.

Dixon called out the commander and crew of the last tank and told them to eliminate the tread tracks from the highway all the way down the lane.

"Break off some branches with plenty of leaves on them. Not near the lane where the breaks can be seen. Go back into the forest a little. Then use them like brooms and wipe out the tracks. I want that done now—even before you rig camouflage."

He waited until he was sure they understood what he wanted. When the elimination of the tracks was progressing well, he walked briskly along the line of tanks until he reached his own. Already the camouflage nets were spread. From the air no trace of the tank force could possibly be seen and from the ground, only an accidental encounter or a prowling patrol would find them. Dixon hauled himself aboard his own tank.

The hatches were all open and the men were waiting for something to happen. Dixon reached down into the main turret and found his map. He spread it on the tank and studied it intently. They were in a fine place, four miles from any town or village. The whole area had been given over to farming, but there weren't enough men left to farm, so this entire section hadn't been fully in seed for two years.

His field phone buzzed and he reached down for it. Colonel Hagen was on the wire.

"Report to the Command Car, Sergeant, on the double."

Dixon slid down to the ground, trotted briskly to the jeep and saluted smartly. He doubted there was another man alive whom he could hate this much and yet salute. It was the Colonel's technical ability and wisdom which made it easy.

"Take a small patrol, well armed, and reconnoiter the village called Avis on the map. Find out if it's being held, if the people there are sympathetic to the Germans. Find out from them, if possible, where the Germans are in this area. Be back here by 0830 hours or we'll send out a relief patrol to see what happened to you."

"Yes, sir," Dixon said.

"Good luck, Sergeant."

"Yes sir, Colonel." He couldn't bring himself to thank this son of a bitch.

Dixon returned to his tank and called the crew down. "I need a patrol to check on a village. You guys want it?"

"Sure," Sal Monda said. "Maybe there's a dame in town, huh?"

"There just might be," Dixon said. "But if you so much as make a pass, I'll clout you one. Okay—BAR's, side arms and grenades. Snap it up."

"Now I know why we got all them guns," Carter said, "I knew this would be a fuggin' job."

"Stay here if you like," Dixon said. "I don't want any gripers with me."

"You couldn't drive him away," Sal Monda said.

Dixon didn't know these men well. Before this foray was over, he'd know them, clear down to how many times a day their bowels moved. But now he had to take his chances. At least they worked well as a unit and so far he hadn't seen any evidences of cowardice. Carter's mild gripe was routine stuff.

"Let's go!" Dixon slung his BAR over his shoulder and walked into the forest. His men followed in single file and he kept moving in a straight line. Dixon knew forests. He'd lived in them, fought in them and made love in them. Lois had been a gamekeeper's daughter in Maine. She used to say she hated the trees and the wilderness, but he'd never believed she really did. He forced her out of his mind quickly.

They reached the edge of the forest twenty-five minutes later and Dixon motioned them down while he scanned the sloping hillside for signs of life.

This was a farm under a good crop. Beans, he figured, though he wasn't certain about those things. There wasn't a living soul within sight.

The village should lay about half a mile behind this sloping hill and in a lush valley. It might be a quiet place which had escaped the shooting war somehow and been allowed to exist by its German captors, because it grew food and the Germans needed it badly.

"Stay here," Dixon ordered. "I'll signal from the top of the slope. If anythin' happens, cover me. If we get caught, we're a doughfoot patrol that got lost and we been wanderin' around for days. We don't know where we are. Got that?"

They all nodded. Dixon wondered how many of them could take it if the Germans questioned them with some of the methods he'd heard firsthand about in Africa.

He figured Kiley could take it. He was intelligent and without even knowing it to be true, figured him as a teacher or a student. Sal Monda was too young. He'd break quickly enough. Amory was a serious type, constantly worried, which meant he was either married or hoped to be as soon as the war was over. You never could tell about his kind. Of Carter, the one who beefed, Dixon thought he'd spit in the eye of his interrogator as they killed him. All in all, it wasn't a bad crew.

He cleared the brush and began running up the slope. He held his BAR at his hip and he was prepared to open up at the sight of the first gray uniform.

He made the rim of the slope and dropped on his belly, crawled the remaining three or four yards and lay there gazing down at the village.

It was a mile away, not a half mile. You never could depend on these GI maps. It seemed to be peaceful enough until he scanned the square through his glasses. Now he could see the motorcycles the Germans depended on so much—and there was one of their gray command cars parked and empty. He couldn't see any soldiers on the single street or in the square, so he estimated this must be a small garrison, probably of specialized troops. It would be easy to take with a couple of tanks, but he didn't know if it was worth the effort.

True, Colonel Hagen had said this force was to make as much trouble and smash as much property as possible, but it seemed a waste to even throw a single shell into this village.

There were no signs of war. The Germans must have simply moved in and met no opposition. The whole damned country must have fallen apart, Dixon thought.

He saw her a moment later. She was a considerable distance away, but she was running over a farm road through the fields. She wasn't heading for the village, but directly away from it. He clamped binoculars to his eyes. She was slim and youthful looking, though certainly not a girl. You could tell that even from this distance—and she was scared. Her head was thrown back and her face a mask of terror.

Dixon moved the glasses and caught the small German car as it came over a ridge and rolled fast down the farm road. There was one man in it—an officer, Dixon thought. He wondered what this was all about.

The car gained on the girl easily. She looked over her shoulder, saw it and turned off the road onto the softer dirt, hoping to escape that way.

The small car wasn't heavy enough to bog down. It rolled past the girl, braked, backed up. She turned in another direction and this time she was headed straight toward Dixon and, quite likely, the forest where she might lose this man.

He picked up the BAR at his side. He didn't know what this was all about, but it was interesting to watch. The officer swung the car to follow her. He drove alongside her, braked, jumped out and went after her on foot.

They were not more than twenty yards away from Dixon now and getting closer. If she topped the ridge and the officer followed, Dixon would be spotted. He figured a burst fired here might not be heard. In any event, he'd certainly have to shoot.

The girl's stamina was giving out fast. She almost fell once. The German could have caught her if he wished, but he matched his speed to hers, tiring her until she tripped and started to fall.

He made a dive for her then, bore her to the ground, wrestling her shoulders down. Neither one of them uttered a sound. It was like a silent movie.

He tore at her blouse, ripped it open and brought his face down to her breasts. At the same time he was covering her body with his own.

Suddenly she began to fight and then silence was broken when he laughed out loud. He tore at her skirt. His knee drove between her legs and he was using one hand to open his fly.

She stopped fighting him. All the strength had gone out of her. She lay there unresisting, panting like an animal just brought down. Her eyes were tightly closed, one hand was at her mouth, knuckles against her teeth.

The German suddenly noticed a pair of booted feet beside him. He looked up in sudden terror. Dixon bent down, grabbed him by the collar, hauled him to his feet. Dixon's knife was in his right hand.

"*Auf Widersehen*, Lieutenant," he said, and slashed upwards with the knife. The point of it entered the German's chest wall and found the heart directly. The German gasped once and slid to the ground. Dixon yanked the knife free, bent down and slit the man's throat.

The woman—he saw now that she was no girl looked up at him in fresh horror, as if this rape was simply passing from one man to another. Then she noticed the uniform and the horror turned to disbelief.

"*Mam'selle*," Dixon said. "I am *Americain. Comprendez . . . ? Americain*."

"Of course," she said in English, well accented but easily understandable. "But . . . where did you come from? How did you get here?"

He bent down to help her up and she cringed away from him in an automatic response to what his extended hand could mean.

"I'm sorry," he said in English. "I scared you. Look —we can't stay here. Will you come with me?"

She got to her feet. "But yes, of course." She brought the edges of her blouse together and patted at her wrinkled, dirt-soiled skirt.

"This Kraut—who was he?"

"A horrible man. They are all horrible."

"Is he important? Will he be missed?"

"I do not think so, Sergeant." She noted his stripes. "He is usually missing when they look for him."

Dixon slung his BAR over his shoulder, bent down and picked up the German lieutenant. He balanced him over one shoulder and moved on down to the small German car.

He placed the dead man over the fender, motioned

the woman into the car and he slid behind the wheel. He sent the small car rolling up the slope over the top of it and hoped to hell his crew didn't have itchy trigger fingers. Just to make sure, he braked, got out and waved both arms. Carter came out of the brush, his BAR ready and he didn't lower it until the car was beside him.

His jaw dropped when he saw the woman. "Where'd she come from?" he asked.

Sal Monda came into the open, gawking like a fool kid. Kiley moved out, but stood there. Amory didn't even look at her. He was scanning the slope just in case they'd have company.

"Monda," Dixon said brusquely, "put your eyes back in your head and get this car and the dead man deep into the woods. I don't want them found, understand? Kiley—escort this lady to the Colonel. She speaks good English and she's a lady. All of you got that?"

"*Merci,*" the woman said with a faint smile.

Kiley nodded and the woman walked beside him. Sal Monda was half in, half out of the German car. Dixon raised a foot and booted him in.

"Kids," he grumbled aloud, "don't know when to look or when to close their eyes. Let's go—I got something to report."

FIVE

Kiley took the woman's arm gently and guided her over the rougher part of the trail, through the forest. They were silent until they reached more open areas where they could walk side by side again.

"Your sergeant," she said, "he is a very good man, *non?*"

"Fine man, *Madamoiselle.*"

"*Monsieur,*" she corrected him, "it is *Madame.*"

"I see," Kiley nodded understandingly.

"Would you be so kind as to tell me his name that I may address him properly when I thank him?"

"I'm sorry, *Madame.*"

She smiled. "You cannot answer, eh? You are not sure of me. Well, that is to be understood. Yet we should not walk in complete silence. Or is that necessary?"

"No, *Madame,*" Kiley said with a grin. "I don't mind telling you my name. It's Terence Kiley and I'm from the central part of the United States."

"Ah, you are a farmer then?"

"A teacher," he said. "Or I hope to be. They pulled me out of college to fight this war."

"That is a calamity, *non?* But you will go back to it and perhaps be a wiser teacher."

"I hope so."

"Is it permitted to tell me where you are taking me?"

"No, *Madame.*"

"Very well. This sergeant of yours, is he always so . . . so impetuous?"

"I don't know what you mean," Kiley said. She smelled faintly of some heavy French perfume. He hadn't smelled perfume in months. His skin began to tingle and he found himself taking somewhat painful sidelong glances toward her breasts, only partly covered by the blouse her hand held together.

If she noticed, she gave no indication of it. "The sergeant, he wished the German officer *auf Wiedersehen* and then killed him quickly."

"He's trained to do that, *Madame.* Frankly, he's only been with our . . . that is, our outfit for a couple of days and we don't know him very well."

"The German was attempting to rape me," she said without any emotion in her voice.

"I'm sorry you had to go through that."

"Yes . . . it was not pleasant, but not the first time either. They are beasts. Are you married, *mon ami?*"

"No . . . not yet." He looked at her directly and with considerable interest now that she sought to share his problems. "I've got a girl though and it's serious. She making plans now to build us a house."

"Ah—*bien!* To come home from the wars and find a new wife and a new home all ready. That should be incentive for you."

"Certainly is," he admitted. "Now—ah—*Madame*, we're coming out of these woods in a minute and—well—there'll be a lot of men around . . . and maybe you'd like to well, sort of fix up a little. . . ."

"Would that be possible?" she asked eagerly.

"Sure—just walk off there behind those shrubs. Come back when you're ready."

"You trust me that far?" she asked with a smile.

"*Madame*, you heard the sergeant say you were a lady. Sergeants are never wrong. I'm not worried about you."

She moved out of sight and quickly managed to tuck the torn blouse under the band of her skirt, bring the edges together and keep them there with the help of one button which had been torn off. She ran fingers through her hair, fluffing it out. It was brownish red, softly waved by nature, cut a medium length and framed her face nicely. She was a beautiful woman.

Kiley was positive of this as she returned to his side, walking with an easy grace that not many women possess. Quite impulsively, because she liked and trusted him, she linked her hand under his arm. The close association made Kiley grit his teeth a little and wish he could see Julie soon.

Then they came out onto the forest road and she saw what seemed to be an endless line of tanks. The crews, all confined to the vehicles, clambered out of the turrets and sat gazing in awe at her. Kiley let his free hand touch hers which still rested on his arm. She smiled and permitted him to leave it there.

They reached the communications truck in which Colonel Hagen had set up a small office. He stared out at them from the canopy and then came to stand on the tailboard. He gravely saluted the woman.

"*Bonjour, Mam'selle*," he said. "Who is she, soldier?"

"I don't know, sir. Sergeant Dixon found her. Some Kraut officer was—ah . . . attacking her and Sergeant Dixon killed him."

"Help her onto the truck, soldier." Hagen reached down a hand to offer his help too. The woman stood on the tailboard beside Hagen.

"*Merci*, my very kind friend," she told Kiley. "I will remember you in my prayers."

"Thank you, *Madame*," Kiley said somewhat uncertainly. "Thank you very much."

He saluted Hagen and turned away. Hagen smiled at the woman. "Won't you sit down, please? We haven't much to offer in the way of comforts here, but you're welcome to what we have."

"*Merci*. You too do not regard me as a spy, then?"

"I don't think so, but I am sure you'd like to tell me about yourself."

She sat down on one of the folding chairs. Hagen offered her a cigarette which she took as it if were a jewel. "It is good of you, Colonel. I have not smoked a fine cigarette for many months."

He lit it for her and she took a deep puff and smiled. "Good . . . *bien!* Now I shall talk, eh? My name is Guillaine Chaumont. I am from Paris. Many months ago I was caught here in a sudden German advance. We did not expect it because the war was in a state of . . . I think your newspapers called it 'the phony war' or the *sitzkrieg* . . . or something like that."

"Yes, I remember."

"So I was caught and they never permitted me to return to Paris. I . . . that is, my family has maintained a chalet here in the country for many years. This is a valley good for grapes, you understand . . ."

His eyes lighted up. "You are of the Chaumont wine family?"

"So you know our wines," she said happily. "That is wonderful."

"Just what happened today?" he asked.

"Oh—yes. Well, our little village was not regarded as a thing of importance. We were ordered to grow no more grapes, tear out our vines and raise beans and carrots and potatoes. We were occupied by an aging ex-postmaster as *gauleiter* and a handful of soldiers. It wasn't too unpleasant. Sometimes, except for lack of cigarettes, coffee and food, it was hard to realize we were occupied and defeated. That changed two weeks ago."

"I see. Just how . . . is it *Madame* Chaumont?"

"*Oui.* I am a widow, Colonel. My husband was killed very early in the war."

"I'm sorry."

"These new Germans moved in. They are engineers and they have been very busy pouring concrete for new walls to our farmhouses. They are turning each building into a fortress and building pillboxes. They have some old tanks dug in. I think that is how you say it. They seemed to expect you Americans very soon."

"How many soldiers are there now?"

"I would say fifty or sixty. The officers, there is a

major in charge, are billeted in my chalet. That is how it came about this young lieutenant . . . tried to make his filthy advances until I was compelled to run away. Oh, if he had not done so, the others would have. I ran . . . he caught me and your sergeant came out of nowhere and it was over."

"I'm glad he got there in time," Hagen said. He found himself admiring her hair and her cool gray eyes, the cut of her chin and the near-perfect outlines of her face.

"I am in agreement, Colonel."

"You'll be safe here. We'll get you behind the lines somehow."

"You will not attack the village?"

"I hardly think it's worthwhile, do you?"

"For the possession of the village, perhaps not, but there is a circumstance . . ."

"Yes?"

"Five days ago someone shot a German soldier. It was a foolish assassination. They promptly arrested fifty men of the village and for the past two days they have shot ten of them each day. Ten more will be shot this afternoon and they say they will keep this up until the assassin comes forward or is produced for punishment."

Hagen rubbed his chin. "I see. And they are fortifying the houses?"

"And—barricading the streets. They intend to make you fight for the village, Colonel."

"You want me to attack, don't you?"

"Would it be possible, *mon* Colonel?"

He shook his head. "We're here to perform

specific work, *Madame*. A small village, fortified or not, is hardly worth risking the success of our expedition . . ."

"But men will die."

"If we attack, more than ten will die," he reminded her.

"*C'est vrai* . . . that is true. Can you tell me what all these tanks intend to do? As I understand it, you are many miles ahead of your own lines."

"Why do you ask?"

"You are suspicious of me," she chided mildly.

"No . . . it's not that, but something in your voice, your expression . . . I don't know what it is . . ."

"There can be only one reason why such a force is secretly this far ahead of the front," she said. "You intend to attack something, somewhere, but you are hiding until night before you advance. Colonel, if I could tell you of a way through forests, over fields, along muddy streams . . . where only a madman would drive a tank battalion like this . . . and make the way perfectly safe for you, then could we bargain?"

He drew a sharp breath. "You'll have to expound that statement further."

"I will. Oh, what's the matter with me? I am not a military person. All I know I learned from General Quetain who is my good friend and who is at my chalet."

"A French General . . . there with the Germans . . . ?"

"*Oui*, but they are not aware of who he is. You see, when they came, the General who had been my guest, became my servant. He is very old and I said he was a valued retainer who has been in the family service a lifetime. They did not question it for he no longer looks like a general."

"All right—what about him?"

"He has always been a student of military problems. I speak like this because for two years we have amused ourselves by planning army movements and maneuvers. In his studies the General ran across an amazing thing. Something we French could have known about, but very few of us do. It is a road, Colonel . . . a long road. . . ."

"You're not being explicit, *Madame*. Please. . . ."

"I am sorry. Many years ago the Normans prepared for invasion and built a network of brick and stone roads all over this area. Some of them extend for many miles and mostly all skirt cities, even go through them. The roads are hidden by time. The earth has been thrown over them, grass covers them, sometimes huge trees grow from them, but they are there and they are strong. They will sustain a tank force."

Hagen leaned forward and placed his hands firmly on both her shoulders. "You're sure of this?"

"The maps are hidden at my chalet. You shall have them, but first you must drive the Germans out."

"An all-weather road," Hagen said. "I heard of it during the first World War."

"You were fighting in that one also?" she asked in amazement.

"I was there," he said grimly. "I have heard of these roads. *Madame* Chaumont, you have done us a great service. I shall attack your town and inflict as little harm on it as possible. Perhaps no shots will be fired if the Germans are sensible."

"You will do this in time to save the next ten from execution?"

"I promise. Someone has to warn the townspeople. Will you do this?"

"Gladly, Colonel."

"Good. I'll have you escorted back to where you were found. Go to the town and tell the townspeople that when we appear, they are to go to their cellars or lie upon the floor in case there is shooting. It should be over in a matter of minutes."

"You will be there soon, then?"

"How far is it?"

"Perhaps five kilometers . . . by the road which brought you to this forest."

Hagen consulted his watch. "It's 1500 hours. In forty-five minutes."

"It will be very close . . . a shame if you do not arrive in time. . . ."

Hagen made up his mind promptly. "I'll send a detail of sixty men on foot, over the fields. You can lead them. They'll let you reach the village, give the alarm and then they'll move in fast. The tanks will come behind them." Hagen stood up and went to the tailboard. "Find Sergeant Dixon," he called. "On the double."

Dixon arrived in two minutes. Hagen handed *Madame* Chaumont down with his help.

"The lady will lead you back to the village, Sergeant. Take sixty men. Close in; attack only after you're discovered and make certain that ten French prisoners are not executed as scheduled before you take the town. It's being fortified, but the work hasn't been completed. Twenty tanks will have the town ringed as you begin your battle. You'll have to improvise. Sergeant, and Major Ballard will be in command. Send someone to find him. He's somewhere down the road, inspecting the rear tanks. Take the jeep."

Dixon saluted smartly, ran to the jeep and Guillaine Chaumont clambered into the seat beside him.

"I have not yet thanked you, Sergeant."

"No need to," he said gruffly. "Fill me in, will you?"

She gave him the details she'd submitted to the Colonel, not including the ancient Norman roads. That could come later. She described the town, and as he had already observed it, he knew how the attack should be launched.

He found Major Ballard, turned the jeep over to him and then called Kiley.

"Take the lady back where we found her. Stay there; we'll join you. She's returning to the village."

In ten minutes Dixon had sixty heavily-armed men deploying through the forest and twenty tanks were pulling out under a lieutenant's direction. They'd make a wide sweep and come down from all sides if possible, to trap the Germans who tried to escape. Dixon estimated that it wouldn't be a big fight, but it might be a brisk one. He wished he had more time, but *Madame* Chaumont had emphasized the importance of preventing the executions.

Dixon wasn't too sure of Major Ballard. He didn't strike the experienced sergeant as a combat officer, even though he'd do his best. But then, what officer equalled the non-coms anyway, Dixon asked himself. Sergeants ran the army. Everyone knew that. Ballard would give the order to attack. After that, nobody would need more orders. Ballard would have to take care of himself from then on.

Dixon reached the edge of the forest where Kiley waited. The woman had already topped the ridge and was probably in town by now. Dixon made his way to the side of the Major.

"I've already scouted that slope, sir. There's nothing on the other side except farms and they lead right down to the village itself. The Krauts don't seem to have any outposts or guards. I guess they feel pretty safe."

"How much clear territory do we have to cover before we start shooting, Sergeant?"

"Too much, for all these men to move over. With your approval, I'm going to send them ten at a time, in small forays, with order to hug the dirt the closer they get to the village. We haven't much time, sir."

"Yes, I know. Colonel Hagen briefed me. Very well, your thinking seems very good. Go ahead, Sergeant."

"Thank you, sir. I'll go with the first ten men."

He selected them quickly, gave them their orders, and let the others listen in. Then he and his squad moved up that slope quickly, but taking care to raise no dust.

Dixon passed the spot where he'd knifed the German and he suddenly wanted to kill more of them. He remembered the bestial violence of the man, his abject terror as he died too. If the officers raped openly, the men must be even worse. Killing Krauts seemed a good thing. Dixon was unconsciously building himself up for violence.

They topped the ridge, looked down at the quiet town. Dixon waved his arms and the men spread out. Each had a BAR, a .45 automatic and enough grenades. Already three more waves were coming up the slope. Dixon signaled for the advance.

They might be seen at any moment, but it really didn't matter too much. The fast-moving tanks must be already encircling the village and ready to close in at the first shot. Before they reached the edge of the fields, Dixon heard one formation of tanks roaring down the highway. They'd be the direct assault group; the others would come as even more of a surprise to the Germans.

Dixon rested the BAR against his hip, stood up and started running. The others followed. If they were seen, to hell with it. You fought a war on your feet, not your belly.

SIX

DIXON AND his ten men reached the rear of one thatch-roofed house without being seen but now, at this close range, they could watch the Germans busily thicken-

63

ing the walls of some of the houses and two tanks were already buried at the far end of the square. Their guns could sweep the street and destroy any tanks that moved toward them.

Dixon looked back. Another wave of ten was running, bent over, trying not to create any dust on the dry ground. The third ten were getting ready to move and behind them was the main force of thirty men. Ballard was with these. Wisely, the Major was letting Dixon take command. So long as he wasn't present with the first squads, he couldn't give any orders, so Dixon was free to act.

Dixon saw a German officer—he seemed to be a captain—emerge from a building that looked like the Town Hall. He was a strutter—he marched, instead of walked, and he surveyed the town as if it were his own.

Dixon drew a bead on him, pulled the trigger, and a dozen heavy slugs threw the officer forward. He'd never even seen the face of his enemy.

Instantly men came pouring out of the Town Hall which had apparently been turned into a barracks. There were more than a dozen of them, hastily trying to figure out what had happened. Dixon's squad cut loose. Four of the Germans managed to escape the hail of death and raced into houses and soon began shooting from the windows.

More men moved out of other houses, but ducked back before they could be killed. Windows were broken, rifles protruded. One of the men in Dixon's squad began running toward a passageway between houses. Two rifles zeroed in on him and he went down.

Dixon swore loudly. They'd have to wait now until the tanks moved in and then those houses were going to have to be blasted one by one. This was already a fortified town and the element of surprise was now lost. They'd have to take it the hard way. He signaled Ballard who came up with his men. The Major took in the situation, ordered his men to fan out and shoot anything in a German uniform. Dixon turned his attion to a hill far to the left of the town. Topping it was the Chaumont chalet. Most of the officers would be there.

"Major, sir," he called and Ballard signaled him to come over. Dixon crawled across a cleared space. Twice the ground was pocked by rifle bullets. So far, no machine guns had opened up, though there was every reason to believe the fortified houses contained them. The Germans simply didn't have any targets to shoot at, or else the guns had not been set up.

"The house up there," Dixon pointed. "Kraut officers are occupying it. They'll try to make a break for it. I suggest I take some men and clean 'em out."

Ballard was peering down a lane which ended in the town square. The same gray command car was still there. Ballard signaled a dozen men to follow him. At first Dixon didn't know what he was up to and then it was too late to do anything about it. Ballard was going to get that car and use it to reach the chalet in time. It was a wild, crazy, impossible thing. The Germans would be watching that car like hawks.

Ballard wasn't even carrying a BAR. He started firing his .45 as he cleared the lane and came into the open. Four men were directly behind or beside him. The Kraut machine gunners had waited. They opened up as Ballard neared the car. Two bursts from those guns and the Major went down. So did all the men close to him.

Dixon yelled in rage and started shooting at the windows where the machine guns were emplaced. This was a hell of a way for a tanker to be fighting a war. This was doughfoot stuff.

"Cover them goddamn windows," he ordered. "I'm going to get the Major if I can."

"Let's go, Sarge." Carter was at his side.

"Where the hell are the tanks?" Dixon looked around. They must still be deploying to seal off any hope of escape from the town. It was best that way. Dixon signaled, his men brought their BAR's to bear on the windows of every house that fronted the street toward which Dixon was running. They succeeded in holding down the machine gun posts, but not the riflemen in other windows.

Bullets zinged unpleasantly past them, but Dixon and Carter raced on. Dixon saw a German lean out a window and draw a bead. He stopped, raised the BAR and riddled him. That quieted some of the other windows.

He reached the Major, flung himself down, grabbed the officer around the middle and rolled with him behind the gray command car. Ballard was alive, but Dixon didn't have to examine his wounds to know he had very little time left. It was apparent the other men were dead.

Carter also knelt beside Ballard. The Germans were trying to pick them off, but the car made a good shield.

"Reach up," Dixon said, "and get the rear door of

the car open. We're going to ease him inside and then try to take off."

"Sergeant," Ballard whispered, "what the hell are you trying to do, give up your life for a dead man? Get out of here."

"Sorry, sir."

"Sergeant . . . listen to me. I'm no combat soldier. I never was, but since I got it—the Big One—let me die like a combat soldier. Give me your BAR. Prop me up a little. Then you drive the car away from here—whatever in hell you want it for. I'll cover you."

"No sir," Dixon said.

"I'm ordering you to do this," Ballard said. His voice was strong enough to be firm. "Do it!"

Dixon glanced at Carter who nodded briefly and shifted the wad of plug he chewed to the other side of his mouth. He spat noisily. Then he reached up, opened the rear door of the car, hoisted himself up a little and managed to drag out the back seat cushion. He placed this so the Major could lean on it to support himself and the BAR.

"All the comforts of home, sir," Carter said.

"Thanks, soldier. Get on with it, Sergeant."

Dixon picked up the Major's .45, tucked it down his belt. He drew his own side arm, snapped off the safety. He opened the front door of the car. He crawled up, wiggling himself into a cramped position, hoping no Kraut was in some upstairs window from which he could watch this operation.

Carter's cold eyes shifted from one house to another. He saw a flash of gray and his BAR smashed through a window. He started spraying all the windows then and from the edge of town, fifty odd men began to do the same thing.

"Now!" Dixon yelled. Carter vaulted into the back of the car, slammed the door. It started quickly, one important break. A stalled motor would have been disastrous.

The car began to move, gained speed rapidly and as it cleared the parking space, Ballard lay there fully exposed, his BAR sweeping the windows.

Two soldiers came barreling out of one house to try and stop the car. Ballard got them. Those were the last shots he fired. About ten rifles zeroed in on him. All the watching tankers could see were the little puffs of dust that arose as each bullet hit.

Dixon roared down the street with wide-open throttle, while Carter stood up in back and kept his BAR working. When the clip was empty, he started using his .45 and when that clip was empty, he started lobbing grenades. There wasn't time to reload.

He never once ducked for cover, never flinched when the car was hit. Dixon had time to notice only part of this, but what he did see told him that Carter was one of those rare soldiers who never experienced true fear. His mind was too intent on killing the enemy to feel any of the terror of being shot at himself.

They saw the tanks closing in and Carter was still standing, waving his arms to signal that while the car might be Kraut, the men in it were American tankers.

Dixon heard the first of the 75's cut loose and the chatter of the 50 mm machine guns. The town wasn't going to be taken easily, but it would be taken soon.

They were clear of the town now and roaring up the dirt road to the chalet. Dixon wondered if the woman was there or if she'd taken refuge in one of the village houses. He had the accelerator pressed to the floor. If anything happened to her, he was going to shoot every goddamn Kraut he met.

Carter crawled over into the front seat and settled himself down. He was laughing loudly. "Y'know somethin', Sarge? This is a pretty good war after all."

He began inserting a fresh clip into his BAR and another in his .45. Dixon didn't answer him. They were close to the chalet now. Dixon braked so hard the car skidded around until it faced the village from which they'd come.

"Jeeze," Carter yelled, "you can get a traffic ticket for that."

"Let's go," Dixon said. He pulled his .45 free, stepped out of the car and made a run for the high stone pillars to which the gate to this country estate was fastened.

Somebody started shooting from inside the house. Dixon dived for the protection of one pillar. Carter stayed with the car, hiding beside it. He saw the broken window through which the automatic rifle had been fired. He watched the curtains intently. One of them was drawn back slightly. Carter sent a hail of steel through the window. Someone, in falling, pulled the curtain down with him. Carter spat tobacco juice and sprayed bullets through several other windows, while Dixon sprinted up the path to the front porch.

Once Dixon was secure, Carter made a beeline for the pillar which had protected the sergeant. There he waited. Dixon kicked in the front door. Somebody fired a burst, but Dixon had leaped nimbly aside, expecting this. An officer with an automatic rifle came rushing onto the porch. Carter killed him with a burst. He shot at the other windows on the first floor, raised the rifle to cover those on the second and gave them a burst. Then he started running, as Dixon had, but Carter had no covering fire. Still, he made it. The kind of bulletheaded luck that accompanies soldiers of his breed, stayed with him. He stood beside Dixon, breathing heavily.

"Goddamn lousy way to fight a war," he said between breaths. "They didn't train us for this. Hell, since when'd we get to be doughfeet?"

Dixon grinned. "At least we know how a doughfoot feels now. And especially when the dough sees a tank coming. Look around."

One of the Shermans was waddling toward him. It was too wide to go through the gate so it knocked down the ancient stone pillars and never faltered. It rolled to a stop; the 75 traversed until it was aimed squarely at the house.

Dixon stuck his head around the corner of the front door.

"*Alles* is *kaput*, you Krauts," he yelled. "Come outa there!"

"*Kameradin*," someone called. A Captain moved out of the living room with his hands clasped at the back of his head. His shoulder was matted with fresh blood.

Carter rammed his belly with the muzzle of the BAR, shoved him against a wall and searched him. Then he grasped him by the back of his jacket and threw him out the front door for the tank boys to take care of.

There was a lot of firing in the village, but neither Dixon nor Carter paid any attention to it. They had problems of their own. They flushed an old retread soldier out of the dining room and ran him onto the porch. The kitchen was a shambles of filth and dirt. The Germans didn't wash dishes, they broke them. Half-eaten food was thrown to the floor. A dead dog, shot through the head, lay in one corner, its teeth still bared in the snarl that had brought on the hatred of the Germans.

Dixon went to the bottom of the staircase. "Up there, you Krauts," he called. "In twenty seconds we'll put a shell through you. Come down here or you'll get yourself killed."

A German Major appeared at the top of the stairs. He was nattily dressed and haughty, as if he were on parade in Berlin. He walked down the steps slowly, a half sneer on his face, but his hands raised shoulder high.

"Take him, Rod," Dixon said. "I'll check the bedrooms."

The German officer, on his way down, refused to move aside for Dixon as he raced up the stairs. Dixon shoved him against the wall, went on by. Carter waited, with the BAR trained and ready. The officer began descending the steps again.

Dixon found that one of the bedrooms had been set up as an office. There were maps and papers and a field telephone there. He didn't stop to check the papers. That could be done later.

He found the old man in another bedroom. He'd

been struck on the head so hard that his skull was shattered. He was dead, but his body was still warm. Dixon made sure there was no one else upstairs and then he walked down to where the Major stood, glaring at Carter.

Dixon walked up to the Major and gently put the muzzle of the .45 against his throat.

"There's an old man up there. Who killed him?"

"I do not know," the Major said in passable English.

Dixon saw the Luger stuck in Carter's belt. He pulled it free.

"Hey," Carter said testily, "that's my souvenir."

"You get it from this crumb?"

"Yeah . . . took it from his holster."

"The butt's all smeared with blood," Dixon said. "The old man had his brains busted out with his gun. Major, do you deny that?"

"I deny nothing. I'm a prisoner. You can do nothing to me."

Dixon said. "That's your big trouble, you miserable Nazi. You don't think we've got the guts for it. It must have taken a hell of a lot to smash the old man's skull. There was no reason for it. He was at least ninety . . ."

"He tried to attack me," the Major said, suddenly losing some of his arrogance. "He kept screaming that he was a general . . ."

"So you busted him. I didn't see any weapon in his hands. I say what you did was murder. What would you say, Rod?"

"Sure . . . murder any way you look at it."

The Major backed away until the wall stopped him.

"You will not kill me . . . you talk of murder . . ."

"You talk too much," Carter said. His BAR cut loose. The Major slumped. Carter glanced at Dixon. "Honest, Sarge, he was comin' down the stairs with the Luger in his hand yellin' he was gonna kill me."

"I know," Dixon said. "I saw it happen."

They walked out to the porch, waved to the tank commander and the hatch flew open. The two prisoners were sitting down under the menace of the machine gun. Neither of them showed any ambition to renew the war.

The firing in the village was desultory now, just an occasional blast from a BAR and once the crunching sound of a grenade thrown into some house. Carter clambered onto the back of the tank. Dixon signaled the two prisoners.

"*Raus!*" he yelled. "Move!"

They scrambled to their feet and walked ahead of the tank until it rolled a little faster and then they ran. Dixon and Carter were cheerfully clinging to the back of the Sherman. It rolled down the main street and Dixon saw Guillaine Chaumont come out of one house. He slid off the tank, hit the ground running and kept running until he was standing before her. He touched his helmet.

"I'm glad to see you're safe, ma'am."

"Thank you, Sergeant. It didn't work out as we had planned, I'm sorry to say. When I gave the word, there was a collaborationist present. He informed the Germans, but not in time to stop you."

"Somebody mentioned prisoners who were to be shot . . ."

73

"They are safe—all thirty village men are quite safe. They were locked in one of the fortified houses which gave them much protection."

"Good."

"We are very greateful, Sergeant. There is nothing we of this village would not do to repay."

"All in a day's work." Dixon shrugged off the praise. "That house up there . . . yours?"

"*Oui*. You have been there, *non?*"

He nodded. "The old man up there your father? No . . . he's gotta be your grandfather if he's any relation."

"He is an old friend of my family. A general . . . *oui*, a real French general."

Dixon shook his head. "That's what he told the German Major. I'm very sorry . . . the old general was killed."

She bowed her head and wept silently as she turned away.

Dixon knew it wouldn't help much, but he said it anyway. "The Kraut who killed him is dead."

She went back into the house without turning around. Dixon sighed and then began to inspect the damage. There were nineteen prisoners which his two joined, six more wounded—litter cases. Dixon wondered what they were going to do with them. The dead were laid in a row. He counted twenty-nine Germans and he counted nineteen pair of combat boots protruding from the blankets which covered the dead tankers. Dixon turned away.

He said, "Carter!"

The tank driver slouched over to where he stood. "What's up, Sarge?"

74

"Have one of the tanks take you back to the chalet . . . that's the house where the old man got killed in case your French is as lousy as I think it is. Get the command car we drove up there and move it fast back to our main position. Tell the Colonel what happened and tell him I'm staying here to clean up the mess."

"Right."

Guillaine had emerged from the house in time to overhear the order. She stopped Carter with a hand on his arm.

"Sergeant, is it permitted that this soldier drive me to see the Colonel?"

"Sure—roll back here and pick her up," Dixon ordered.

Carter climbed onto a tank and told the driver to rev it up. Guillaine sat down on the front steps of a nearby house. Dixon stood over her, feeling awkward and foolish. She looked up at him with a smile.

"Please excuse me for sitting down. It has been a hectic day and I am near exhaustion."

"It's okay."

"I have talked to several of the men of the village. We intend to repay for your help. I have news for the Colonel about a large air base not too far away . . . perhaps thirty kilometers. It would make . . . how would you say it? . . . a very nice kill for your tanks."

"It sure would, ma'am. You tell the Colonel and he'll see to it that air base disappears."

"There may be other things we know," she said. "Is it permitted that we bury your dead?"

"We'd appreciate it," he said. "I'll assign a man to collect the dog tags and possessions."

"Yes . . . then we may bury them before dark. It will be in our own cemetery. Their graves will be well-tended and kept green for as long as this village exists. This we wish to do."

"Thank you. I'm sure the Colonel won't object."

"The Germans will have to take care of their own," she said curtly.

"We'll put the prisoners to burying them, ma'am. Don't worry about it."

"No," she said. "No, I shall never again worry about what happens to a Nazi."

She grew silent then, until some of the villagers sought her out and she talked to them in French while Dixon stood politely by. After a few moments Carter roared into town with the command car and Dixon helped Guillaine into the seat beside him.

"See you," he said curtly.

She smiled and nodded as the car roared away. She was seeing Hagen. Sure—she had to. He was the boss. But Dixon had a feeling that Hagen was taking her away from him. It was an odd feeling too, because he knew he had no claim on her and yet he didn't want to yield her to Hagen.

He felt uneasy and angry. He yelled at one of the Kraut prisoners who had lowered his hands from the back of his head to let the blood circulate. That helped somewhat.

SEVEN

COLONEL HAGEN removed his helmet as he walked into the chalet behind Guillaine. The dead Major had been removed, the bloodstains washed from the wall. The old general was to be buried in the morning near the Americans who had given their lives here.

The chalet, under Sergeant Dixon's orders, had been cleaned up completely. By now the tanks were back in their forest hideaway, the tracks of their coming and going, obliterated. A sharp lookout was kept for aerial survey or attack. Word of the raid on the village must have gone out over their telephones long ago, but so far, no counter-measures had been taken. Perhaps the Germans were too busy redoubling their efforts to prepare a formidable resistance to the tank forces when the real attack came.

Dixon was on hand when Hagen and Guillaine arrived. He saluted Hagen, greeted Guillaine respectfully and fell back while she escorted Hagen through the ancient, beautiful home. Then they went to the room which the Germans had turned into a planning room. Hagen and Dixon studied the maps intensively.

"This isn't a bad find," Hagen said. "A rather complete mapping of the villages they're preparing, to slow Patton down after he breaks loose." He opened one large map, indicated a defense in depth. "They're buying time and it'll be costly to us if we have to smash these one by one. However, with what these maps show, perhaps we can avoid some of the traps."

"Maybe blow a few of 'em to hell before we go back," Dixon suggested.

"Possibly. But I'm interested in this airfield. Stukas have been doing a lot of damage to our tanks and supply depots. It would be a help to clean out a whole airfield of them."

"Yes sir," Dixon said. It sounded to him like a suicide attack.

Guillaine placed before Hagen, the ancient maps showing the location of the Norman all-weather roads, hidden for generations beneath a thin layer of soil. The maps were remarkably clear and, correlated with modern maps, it was easy to draw the route of the ancient road as it pertained to modern conditions. The most amazing thing was that one of the hidden roads began close by this village and ran in almost a straight line to a point within a mile of the Stuka base. Most of the route over farmland and idle fields.

Hagen pointed it out to Dixon. "What do you think, Bert?"

Dixon compressed his lips slightly at the use of his first name. He had an urge to tell him he was out of his mind, but a sergeant doesn't question a colonel's decision, even when asked. He gave up.

"We could take off in half an hour, sir. We'd be at the base and back by nightfall. Hit it hard and get cleared away. Knowing this road, we could move a hell of a lot faster'n the Krauts would expect, sir."

78

Hagen nodded. "Report back to Lieutenant O'Connor. Use the extra gas we brought in the truck and fill our tanks as full as possible. Be ready to move out at 1700 hours with the first twenty-five tanks."

"Yes sir."

"That's all, Sergeant."

Dixon saluted, gave Guillaine a thin smile and walked out. She and Hagan heard the command car roar back to the forest where their base of operations was now located.

Guillaine sat down on a chair done in petit point by someone who must have been of the era of her great grandparents. Hagen was folding and stacking the maps.

"Is there something between you and this oh-so-tough sergeant, Colonel Hagen?" she asked.

He smiled. "You noticed it, eh? Well, I suppose it is obvious. Yes, he hates my guts and with what he honestly believes is a proper reason. However, he doesn't let that interfere with being a good soldier. As for me, I need him, especially on this venture. I lost my Major, didn't bring along any captains because they were needed elsewhere, so my remaining officers are a first and a second lieutenant. Good men, but not of Dixon's calibre."

"I hope whatever it is makes the sergeant hate you, will soon vanish so you two may be friends."

"Well, I hope so too, but I don't look forward to it. Not after all these years. Thank you, Guillaine, for your help."

"Mine?" she scoffed. "What have I done? You will go now?"

"Yes, but I intend to come back here. The way I

look at it, the Germans have no idea of the size of our force, where we came from or where we're going. They'll probably figure we're just half a dozen tanks on some sort of patrol and after we cleaned out your village, we must have high-tailed it for home."

Hagen went over to a chair and sat down, his eyes again taking in her beauty. She was wearing a pale green dress and her face was freshly made up, her hair beautifully arranged. She crossed her legs as she talked and Hagen had a hard time keeping his eyes on a level with hers.

"If there is any other way we may be useful, Colonel, you have only to ask."

"I heard you had a collaborator who warned the Germans we were coming."

"That is true. Fortunately, he was unable to give them sufficient notice. The shooting began only a few minutes after he reached the German commandant."

"You took care of him"

"He is dead," she said simply.

"There are no others?"

"We are very certain of that, Colonel."

"Then you can help us. We'll come out of the forest straight onto the Norman Road which is approximately halfway over your farmland and just North of this chalet."

"Yes . . . I could see that on the map."

"If your people would eliminate the tracks our tanks will make so that air observation or even patrol work wouldn't reveal where we came from, it would help."

"I assure you, all tracks will be removed after you go and again, after you return."

"Thank you. This forest where we are so well hidden, is an excellent, centrally located spot from which we can radiate out as we wish and always get home before they can surround us. If the Germans ask in your village, tell them it was only six light tanks which came on the raid and they disappeared back toward our own lines. Make certain the stories of everyone agree."

"I am very happy you will be back, Colonel," she said frankly.

He arose and went to her. He extended his hands and she took them and he gently pulled her to her feet.

"I'm glad too. You're a lovely woman, Guillaine. Much too lovely to be alone like this, without a man's company and love."

"One gets accustomed to it, Colonel," she smiled.

"I don't believe you ever quite did," he said. "I know I haven't. I was married once. My wife has been dead for many years."

She nodded and the smile faded. "*Oui*, I know how it feels to be alone that way. You wish to kiss me, Colonel. It is well. I wish to be kissed."

He drew her to him, enfolding her smooth softness, and the kiss which was at first gentle became demanding and passionate until her arms were clasped around his neck and her body was pressed very hard against his.

They were not children. They were mature people with a need for one another and the sensible frank-

81

ness not to try and hide it. He drew back slightly, still holding her.

"If I come back and you're here—alone—I'll know why, Guillaine."

"Come back," she implored. "You will find me. There is no one else. There never has been since my husband was killed."

"I'm sure of that. I can't stay. Damn this war for getting in our way."

"Hush, Colonel," she whispered. "Think how it interferes with the lives of some soldiers—forever. We will have our day, you and I."

He touched her face. "Frankly, while the war is on, I'm interested in our nights, my dear. Wait for me." He picked up the package of maps, paused to kiss her on the neck and then the lips. He walked out of the chalet as rapidly as he could, not daring to glance around. Dixon had sent the jeep back. Hagen clambered into it and the driver rocketed off toward the road. Hagen watched the sky intently. It seemed odd that there had been no air survey, no sky hunt for the tanks.

They raced down the one-lane road beside the row of tanks. Dixon occupied the commander's seat in the first tank, his helmeted head projecting above the open hatch. Hagen left the jeep only to get his battle jacket and a BAR. Then he climbed back into the jeep, studied the map a moment and signaled the advance.

Twenty-five tanks pulled out. Ten were to remain as a rear guard in case there was pursuit and to guard the German POW's. They were on battalion radio network now. The Germans knew some sort of force had invaded their lines, so radio silence was no longer absolutely necessary, though too much use of it might pinpoint their location.

Hagen's jeep roared down the continuation of this road which bisected the forest, hit the open field and promptly slowed in a few inches of soft soil. He guided the driver to the left until the wheels found substance. The ancient road was there, hidden, but strong enough to support the battalion. Hagen had the jeep stop and by signals he directed Dixon onto it. The other tanks followed precisely. All commanders and drivers knew about the road now. The line of tanks moved out, over the farmland into which the heavy vehicles should have sunk to their turret guns. Instead, they rolled on, slowly at first while Hagen located the hard surface for them and then faster as the road could be more easily seen.

As they roared on up over the brow of a hill onto pasture land where the going would be easier and the hard road not absolutely required, Hagen saw an amazing thing. From the farmland, scores of farmers with rakes and brooms, were moving up behind the tanks and eliminating all traces of their passage.

They were able to maintain a constant speed of twenty-five miles an hour, even through a four-mile section of swampland where they should normally have bogged down. All turrets were open and machine guns were aimed skyward. An enemy plane sighting this line of tanks, would come down to investigate.

Their luck held. Once, when four Stukas came over, the tanks were close to a line of trees so they maneuvered quickly, nosing into the forest in time to escape detection. The Stukas streaked for their airfield and the tanks moved on out with the same destination in mind, but with a completely different purpose.

Hagen was already planning the withdrawal. It would be a lengthy one, but at least they'd be where tanks were not supposed to be and he hoped the Germans would search everywhere but these soft fields. The Norman roads were going to be very useful so long as their existence remained a secret to the Germans.

Hagen's map showed they were three miles from the Stuka base and now their progress became a touch-and-go affair. Planes would be taking off and landing. Just a casual turn of the head and a pilot might spot the tanks. All Hagen could hope for was that the German pilot would be so sure the tanks must be German that he wouldn't bother to investigate.

Hagen's jeep slowed and he looked for a rendez-vous point where the tanks would be fairly well hidden, at least while the airstrip was checked. The fields here were in wheat, most of it quite tall. He signaled Dixon and the sergeant jumped off his tank and hurried to the command car.

"Have the men hand-reap as much of this wheat as possible," he ordered, "so they can cover the tanks with it. I'm going ahead with Lieutenant O'Connor to scout the situation. Make it fast, Sergeant."

Dixon saluted, passed the word along. In fifteen minutes the tanks were covered well enough so that a passing plane would likely see nothing suspicious in the fields below. Dixon, standing on top of his turret, could barely make out the bulges where the tanks were hidden and their path through the wheat was covered. Hagen must have developed this back in the States on maneuvers, Dixon thought.

Hagen and O'Connor, the much-too-young first lieutenant, rode the jeep through the fields until they reached the ridge of the long valley in which the airstrip had been built. They left the jeep covered, like the tanks, two miles back, while they reconnoitered on foot.

Hagen nodded happily at the sight below them. Here the sides of this valley were smooth, not sloped too much and the tanks wouldn't be impeded on leaving. There were enough trees and brush to keep the presence of the tanks hidden for a time and there seemed to be no defenses set up against an attack, beyond the normal ones security demanded.

Mostly the defense ran to antiaircraft weapons, none of them even manned so far as Hagen could determine through his field glasses. He counted seventy Stukas in line formation or undergoing repair near the long sheds. There were barracks, a recreation yard, tanks of petrol and what looked like a good-sized ammo dump.

"Prettiest thing I ever saw, Colonel," O'Connor observed with satisfaction.

"Beautiful, Lieutenant. All ours for the taking. Let's go back and fetch the tanks."

They drove more slowly than they wished, because they didn't want the sound of the jeep to be heard and they had to keep an eye out in the sky for planes. Being spotted now would wreck the operation.

They reached the tanks. The hand-reaped wheat was thrown aside, the tanks began to move out. The closer they got to the valley, the faster they went. After a certain point was passed, it didn't matter if they were discovered.

Hagen left the jeep and climbed into one of the tanks. Lieutenant O'Connor took time to conceal the jeep before he swung aboard another tank, but Dixon's was still the lead and he was now moving at top speed for this kind of terrain. They'd left the Norman road far back, but it would be very useful in their retreat.

They topped the ridge and stormed on down. The file spread into a long line, properly spaced. All hatches were now buttoned up. Those ack-ack guns could be brought down for level firing and they were deadly things.

The element of surprise was all with the tanks however. They weren't spotted until it was much too late to get the guns cranked down for level shooting—or to get planes in the air.

Dixon glued his eyes to the periscope, picking targets and relaying them to Amory at the 75. The radio crackled and Hagen's crisp voice came over.

"Tanks fire at will."

A barrage of shells went screaming toward the line of planes. They had to be eliminated first. Half the tanks waddled in a line along the row of Stukas, blasting them with incendiaries, blowing them up, setting them aflame. It was like peacetime target shooting.

Germans were racing for cover. Not many made it. The machine guns concentrated on them and cut them down. Dixon gave the orders that sent *Daisy* straight toward the petrol supply depot. Amory drew a bead on the largest of the cluster of tanks, fired, and the tank blew up. Flames roared skyward, the heat set off other tanks and the whole gasoline dump went up.

Somebody else fired into the ammo supply and the aerial bombs began to explode. Dixon suddenly threw open his hatch, pulled himself up and added the power of the BAR to the heavy machine gun that was sweeping the barracks.

Pilots were killed as they rushed out. Goering's airforce was going to feel the pinch after this destruction of machine and man power. If Patton and all his tanks had moved into this attack, no one would have been happier than that scrappy general.

They did get two antiaircraft guns leveled off and one of them slit a tank almost in half. Nobody crawled out of the wreckage, but the gun didn't fire again. Four tanks let go simultaneously and wiped out both guns and the crews.

Hagen sat in the open too, peering about through the smoke. Rifle bullets caromed off the tanks frequently, but resistance wasn't much. Hagen checked the damage and saw that it was just about complete.

He picked up his radio. "Command One to all Commanders. Let's get the hell out of here."

The tanks withdrew, still firing at whatever pockets of resistance were left. There weren't many. They turned and waddled up the slope, turrets traversing so the guns covered their rear.

Hagen was cheerfully contemplating a fast run back to their hideaway when the first bomb dropped. A tank, about a quarter of a mile from Dixon's suddenly vanished in a geyser of dirt and steel. Dixon looked up and cursed.

The one thing they hadn't counted on, a squadron of Stukas coming in for a landing to find their field destroyed and the destroyers still withdrawing. The Stukas had been on an unsuccessful patrol, so their guns and bomb racks were loaded.

One of them peeled off, headed down like a rock, the scream of it heard easily above the steady roar of the moving tanks. Dixon grabbed the radio mike.

"Evasion tactics," he screamed. "Evade . . ."

Four more Stukas were peeling off. Dixon slid down, slammed the hatch over his head. There wasn't much they could do. Machine gun antiaircraft firing wasn't much good against these planes which streaked down too fast to keep in range.

Dixon heard their bombs bursting and these pilots and planes were accurate. They didn't release a bomb until they were so close to their target they couldn't miss. The tanks were catching hell now.

Only one thing favored the tanks. The planes had been on a long patrol and their tanks were almost empty. They could attack now, but they couldn't land, refuel, rearm and start another run. There was no field to land on, no fuel and no bombs.

But they kept it up for twenty minutes of agonizing destruction. It was like being depth-bombed in a submarine. You never knew how close the next one would be. You couldn't see the enemy. You just rode it out, praying hard you weren't in the sights of some bombardier.

Through the periscope Dixon saw they were now

in the wheat field and there seemed to be no more crunching explosions. He swiveled the periscope about. Behind him were individual fires—tanks burning. He had no idea how many, but too many even without a count.

Dixon threw open the hatch, pulled himself out and brought his binoculars to bear on the destruction. It was easier to count the burning tanks than the escaping ones. A quick estimate indicated at least ten tanks had it completely and three or four more were staggering along in the wake of the others. There'd be no survivors in the burning tanks, no one to go back for. Dixon had seen the work of the Stukas on tanks many, many times in Africa.

He spotted two Stukas still in the sky, but they were frantically looking for a landing place. He watched one of them take a chance on the wheat field. He was probably out of gas and had little choice. He came down in a great glide, tried to elevate quickly, but a row of trees was in his way. He didn't make it. One wing hit, the plane tipped, nosed down and crashed.

Dixon spat over the side of the tank. At least he had the pleasure of seeing one of those devils get it. The other vanished over the horizon, probably still looking for a place to land. All the others had vanished By now an alarm was out. More planes would come as soon as the Germans could get them in the air.

Hagen jumped off his tank without allowing it to stop. He raced to where he'd left the jeep, roared down the line of tanks, considerably shortened now, and took the lead to probe for the Norman road.

All commanders rode the tops of their tanks and

kept their eyes skyward. Another half an hour . . . a bare thirty minutes . . . that was all they needed. The hard road enabled them to move at thirty-five miles an hour. Luckily, nobody got bogged down and had to be pulled out. Those roads would save them if they had just the grace of these few additional minutes.

They were all across the farmland and the villagers were out in force with their rakes and brooms, erasing the tracks as the first search planes came over, quite low. All tanks were within the forest now.

When the German planes came out of the clouds, the pilots saw only the farmers at work in their fields. When they swept lower, the villagers waved to them and showed no signs of panic. The planes roared on, hunting for a tank force that seemed to have turned into a phantom. The forest they flew over gave no indications that tanks were hidden there.

Dixon observed the planes as they swept off into the distance. He listened for sounds of others, especially some little observation plane which moved slower and should be better suited for closer inspection. Nothing else came over.

It was time to lick the wounds.

EIGHT

Lieutenant O'Connor was dead, back there at the Stuka field, in what was left of his tank. There were nine wounded men, all of them seriously burned. They lay wrapped in blankets, shot with morphine. Nothing more could be done for them here.

Miraculously, none of the tanks had been lost traveling at high speed, moving fast to beat the darkness. Night had closed around them now and they were safe for a few hours. Time to complete their camouflage, so when more planes came over in the morning, they'd be even better hidden from their view.

Men were exhausted—from a day that began long before dawn and included a perilous drive through enemy lines, an attack on the village and then the destruction of the Stuka airfield. A productive day at least—and a costly one.

Colonel Hagen would want to know the price soon. Miller, the second lieutenant, was busy directing repairs on some of the battered tanks, so the paper work fell to Dixon.

His accumulated figures indicated that of the original thirty-five tanks, twenty-three were left. Of these, six were probably done for and would be cannibalized for other less seriously damaged ones.

There was no surplus of men. The village battle had been deadly and the airfield raid cut their forces by eighty-two men. Gas tanks were almost empty, ammunition was at a premium, especially the 75's. They were still a formidable force, but badly hurt.

Dixon made his way to the communications truck and Colonel Hagen asked him aboard. Hagen was writing letters in the shielded light of an electric lantern. Dixon knew whom they were addressed to.

"Too many of them, sir." Dixon indicated the letters.

"Yes," Hagen said curtly. "I see you've made a survey."

Dixon gave him the figures orally and then laid the written report on the folding desk.

"Shall I make plans to rendezvous with a tanker and cargo carrier, sir?"

"Not tonight, Sergeant," Hagen studied the reports.

"Christ," Dixon exploded. "What do we fight with if we're attacked?"

Hagen looked up. "We won't be if we sit still," he said mildly.

"But damn it . . . the wounded and burned men. . . ."

"We'll do our best for them. If we send someone now, or even transmit a radio message, the Germans will likely know about it. How long do you think it would take them to find us?"

"At least, let's get the wounded into the village where they can be cared for, sir."

"No."

"Goddamnit!" Dixon exploded again. He took a long breath. "I'm sorry, sir, but I've got strong feelings about this."

"So have I. Or do you think I've lost all sense of proportion, Sergeant? If we send wounded to the village and Germans come by, every person in the village will be shot and so will our wounded."

"Yes sir, I suppose so," Dixon conceded. "But the ammo situation has me worried."

"Go to bed. Get yourself some rest. We're safe now and we're not going to budge until morning. Send Lieutenant Miller here."

Dixon saluted without exerting himself. "Yes, sir."

Hagen leaned back and permitted himself a smile. "But—we pulled it off though, didn't we? This attack proves that my theories about small armored striking forces behind enemy lines, really work."

"Yes, sir. I won't deny that."

"And we're not finished. Be sure to post guards. This whole area is pretty hot right now."

Dixon jumped off the truck, located Lieutenant Miller, arranged for guard duty and finally crawled into his bedroll and gratefully closed his eyes. From where he lay, he could see Colonel Hagen still at work on his letters. At least he wasn't seeing the French woman.

Dixon pondered his chances with her. No fly-by night stuff, but the real thing. She'd charmed him at once. It had been years since he'd even considered another woman although he'd hardly lived in a state of celibacy—but Guillaine was attractive, mature, desirable and, he thought, democratic enough to consider a tanker sergeant.

If she placed him and the Colonel on an even basis however, there'd be no contest. But if it came to that, Dixon knew how to make the odds turn in his favor. He cursed Hagen softly and tried to sleep.

Colonel Hagen finished his letters, checked maps, gave Lieutenant Miller further orders to keep the camp on an alert basis and get the tanks patched up as quickly as possible. Then he snapped off the electric lantern, eased himself down to his blanket on the bed of the truck, but there was more desire than sleep in him. After half an hour of this, he gave up.

He put his shoes on again, picked up his helmet and BAR and eased himself off the truck silently. He walked faster as he neared the path through the forest. A sentry pointed a gun at him. Colonel Hagen identified himself and the sentry apologized. He was Rod Carter and he watched the Colonel head in the general direction of the village or the chalet. Carter sniggered a little and didn't blame him.

Hagen saw no lights in the chalet, but that was hardly surprising since it was almost midnight. He moved carefully, stopping now and then to listen and observe. When he reached the chalet, he lifted the great bronze knocker and let it drop. He stepped to the side of the door and aimed his BAR at it.

She came at once, as if she might have been waiting in the darkness . . . and perhaps hoping. She opened the door slightly.

"It is you!" she exclaimed when she saw him in the shadows.

"Yes. May I come in?"

"I've been expecting you, Colonel Hagen." She moved aside so he could enter and she closed the door promptly. "How did it go?"

They were in darkness now, but Hagen's eyes were getting used to it. "Very well. We lost tanks and men, but we obliterated that airfield."

"I'm glad. Very pleased. I want this beast of Nazism destroyed as quickly as possible."

"It'll be destroyed. Are you happy that I came?"

She moved toward him, stopped just short of his reach. "Yes . . . I would have been gravely disappointed, my dear."

"You're aware of why I came?"

"*Oui*, for the same reason I am here to meet you and be loved by you."

He held out his arms and she came into them willingly. He held her to him for a long time, letting the desire rise now, not trying to quell it, no longer fighting against it. During that moment in the darkness, he shattered the memories of the past until they barely existed any more and he felt peace and contentment for the first time in years.

He kissed her with all the passion in him and felt her respond until they were both breathless and eager. He picked up helmet and gun, carried them with him to her bedroom upstairs. They were silent because words weren't necessary. In the bedroom it was darker than downstairs, for the thick draperies were drawn, shutting out even the starlight. He removed his battle jacket and his shoes, found that his hands were shaking as he stripped off shirt and trousers and then peeled down to the raw. He couldn't see her, but the perfume and the womanly smell of her drew him to her. He'd heard the faint rustle of clothes but he was, nevertheless, surprised when he reached for her and found her naked.

They moved to the bed, still locked in an embrace, and their first moments of love-making were brief, because there was too much longing, too great a desire. The reaction left them gasping for breath, but with a contentment Hagen had never quite experienced before.

He could see her now, despite the darkness, for his eyes were even more used to it. She lay back, shamelessly exposed, and she smiled at him.

"You will stay the night?"

"As late as I dare."

"Was it as good as you had anticipated?"

"Better. Much better."

"I thought so too. Will this end for us, Luke, when you move on?"

"Not if I can help it. Guillaine, I'm not a man who considers war an excuse to find himself all the women he can. To me, what we did has just as much sanctity in war as it has in peace. I'm in love with you. The answer, you see, is quite simple. I came to you because I love you. That means I want to marry you."

"I know. I was so sure of that."

"I really don't see how it can be managed, but I'll marry you tomorrow if you like."

She turned on her side and placed a smooth hand against his cheek. "But no, Luke. How much more sensible to wait. After all, it is war and it may last a long time. No one can foresee how it will end."

"Oh, hell," he said, "we've got them licked now. All we have to do is make them understand it."

"Of course, but I didn't mean that. So many things can happen to people in war. And if you need me, I shall be here, Luke. I can't take a gun and fight, but I can be here whenever you come back."

"You're wonderful," he said.

"Tell me about your wife," she urged gently. "I'm not prying. I merely wish to know what I have to contend with, for you must have memories of her."

"Yes . . . bitter ones. Some day I'll talk about them, not now. I can promise you this, her memory will never come between us."

"Yet I have a feeling her death hurt you very much."

"She was killed . . . in an auto accident. It did hurt . . . very much. It happened almost fifteen years ago. It's over. Let's not dust off the memories. This is not the time for it."

"Of course," she said sympathetically, "This is a time for our love. Yours and mine. Luke . . . make love to me again. It's been so lonely and so long . . ."

She crept into his arms once more and afterwards they both slept until light found its way through the not-quite-closed draperies and Hagen bounded to his feet. He'd expected to get back to the forest by dawn. It was a good hour beyond that now.

Guillaine had moved and sighed when he shook the bed getting out in a hurry, but she didn't waken. He put on his clothes, except for shoes. He carried these downstairs before he laced them on. Then he took a good long look out of several windows of the first floor, to make sure no Germans had slipped into the village during the night.

Everything seemed to be peaceful. He opened the

front door, moved out, walked rapidly toward a short cut to the forest hiding place for his tanks and felt easy only when the trees and shrubs closed in around him.

The camp was silent, some of the men still sleeping, others morosely eating K rations and thinking about ham and eggs, toast and hot coffee. Sergeant Dixon and his crew were playing cards with a dog-eared boisterousness of the game. When Dixon saw him deck, but they played quietly, without the usual stride down the road toward the communications truck, he threw in his hand and arose.

As Hagen went by, Dixon fell in step with him. "The Colonel has been reconnoitering, no doubt?"

Hagen eyed him coldly. "The Colonel has been seeing a lady, Sergeant."

"Yes sir, and four of the burned men died. Two German prisoners died, the men are getting restless and they're talking doom. You know what that does to troops, sir. They need inspirational leadership. I heard you say that in a lecture, sir. Long time ago."

Hagen faced him when they reached the truck. "One of these days, Bert, you're going to overstep and I'll come back at you in a way you won't like. Send Lieutenant Miller to me."

"He's sick, sir."

"What's the matter with him? He was all right last night."

"I think it's battle fatigue, sir. And a touch of being scared. Last night he found out he seemed to be in command of this outfit and I guess he didn't feel up to it, so he got sick. You know what the medics say . . . psychosomatic stuff. He ain't really sick, he

98

just thinks he is, but that don't make him any less sick."

"That's not crap you're making up because you're sore at me?"

"The Colonel has only to take a good look at the Lieutenant to see it's true."

"All right. Climb aboard."

Hagen was on the truck first, but Dixon disdained the offer of the Colonel's hand to help him climb up. Hagen spread a map on the little table. His finger traced the route they'd used in reaching this point from their own lines.

"I'm going to load the wounded and the prisoners on this truck and send it back to our lines, at the point where we crossed over. I'll need four or five men to handle it. I intended to have Lieutenant Miller lead, but according to your diagnosis, he's out of it. You'll have to take the job, Sergeant."

"Yes sir."

"You'll leave within an hour."

"In daylight?" Dixon exploded. "Listen, last night I wanted to do this . . ."

"Shut up, Sergeant."

Dixon opened his mouth to protest again, but the cold gleam in Hagen's eyes discouraged him. He merely said, "Yes sir."

"If you traveled by night, Kraut patrols would have stopped you wherever they were posted and you can bet there's a lot of them between here and our lines. You wouldn't have had a chance."

"And we do have by day?" Dixon asked. "How do you explain that, sir?"

"Quite simple. You'll have all markings erased from

the truck. Use mud to cover insignia and numbers. Our trucks are not so different from the Germans' that they'll notice. Especially since the staff car we liberated will lead the truck."

Dixon nodded slowly. "I still don't get the whole picture, sir."

"In the truck, seated like soldiers on transport, will be our German prisoners. Let them know if they give any warning, they'll be the first to die. Put a couple in the staff car too. No American soldier will wear any part of a German uniform. Clear?"

"It might work, sir."

"It has to. When you reach position marked Z on the map, stop and send a brief message by radio. If the Germans pick it up, it'll take them awhile to decipher it, but on our side they'll be expecting the call and the frequency will be constantly monitored. You'll then high-tail it for our lines where they'll be waiting."

"And then all we have to do is get back?"

"With the truck loaded with ammo, gasoline and food. Two trucks if you can scrounge them, or three. Get all you can, but no more men or tanks."

Dixon regarded the truck. "We'd better strip the canvas top off so the Kraut prisoners can be seen. I'll take my own tank crew. I'm getting to know them. They're pretty good men."

"Take your pick of anyone. Get this on the road immediately. I'll clean my stuff out of here now."

Dixon put it up to his crew. Anyone who wished to back out, was free to do so. Nobody said a word and Dixon put them to work getting the cargo carrier ready. When they finished, the wounded were put aboard, arranged in rows and partially covered with the canvas top which had been removed from the arched framework.

The German POW's were settled on the benches, given their unloaded rifles and warned that if they made one untoward move at any time, they'd be the first to die if there was shooting. They didn't seem particularly anxious to die for Hitler. Dixon doubted he'd have any trouble.

Kiley would ride in back with them, but prepared to duck under the canvas if they were seen or had to pass enemy vehicles or roadblocks. Carter, riding in front with Dixon driving, would then use the threat of his BAR to keep the Germans cowed.

The staff car which was to precede the truck, would be driven by Monda, an ambulatory German casualty beside him with another in back where Amory would be in control with his BAR.

At the last moment Colonel Hagen called Dixon aside and gave him his final orders.

"For the moment," he said, "let's drop all this personal animosity. We've got an extremely important job to do."

"Yes sir," Dixon agreed.

"All through the years we helped build tank forces in peacetime; we planned for situations like this. They've never been put into operation, never tested under battle conditions. Right now they will be. Get this carrier and the staff car back of our lines. You know how to do that. Boldness is the best method."

Dixon allowed himself a grin. "I remember in war

games, we sent four trucks marked with the Blue Army insignia, right on through the Green Army lines and we never even got off the highway."

"Exactly. I'm not going to say you won't be spotted or you won't run up against a roadblock no one could penetrate, but you may cover a great deal of ground before you have to make a run for it."

"I know how that's done too," Dixon said.

"I'm aware of it. When you reach our lines, tell them what's happened. Get as much in the way of supplies, gasoline, ammo and rations as you can. Two . . . three carriers full. And ask for orders. General Stratton's HQ will know about them. Frankly, no one really believed this would work and what we've done so far has been on more or less of an experimental basis. I know, however, that they've got a Big One on tap for us, if they think we can get away with it."

"Yes sir. I'll report to the General."

"Don't start back until after dark and then make a straight run for it. You'll be loaded. Evasionary tactics won't be easy, so depend on speed if you can."

"Yes sir. We'll make it okay."

"Good luck," Hagen said.

Dixon saw the Colonel's hand move toward him in a gesture of friendship. He stepped back abruptly, saluted and walked away. He climbed aboard the truck and started the motor. The staff car moved out and the truck followed. The tired tankers watched it with apathy, but hope.

Dixon turned onto the paved road and picked up

speed. Carter stuffed a fresh supply of tobacco into the side of his mouth and chewed reflectively.

"Y'know, Sarge, this might work because it's so goddamn crazy, nobody's gonna question it."

"Yeah," Dixon grunted.

"You don't seem excited about it, Sarge. Maybe you don't think we'll get away with it."

"If we do, all of us should rate the Congressional Medal of Honor. Listen, we got nearly thirty miles of driving through Kraut real estate loaded with their men. They know a raiding party raised hell yesterday behind their lines and if it didn't manage to get back, it sure as hell will try to soon. So they'll watch everything. Hell, we're in American uniforms. I'd just as soon we traveled in Kraut uniforms."

"Hey—we'd get shot as spies if we did that."

"Carter, you're goddamn stupid sometimes. If they nail us, do you think they'll just make POW's of us? They'll cut us down as soon as we got nothing left to tell them."

"Yeah . . . it'd be too bad," Carter said, "but I got me a couple of BAR's and plenty of ammo and if they take me, pal, they'll have to climb over a stack of their own dead to do it."

"Big, brave guy," Dixon jeered. "They could get you with one little slug before you had a chance to even lift that BAR you're massaging, as if it was a woman's ass."

Carter grinned. "Been a long time since I rubbed a woman, but the way I remember it, felt a lot like this gun. Smooth, with a lot of potential life in it."

"Let's knock off the chatter. Pay more attention to

103

the road and maybe blocks. Boy, this is some trip."

"You might almost think the Colonel was trying to get rid of us, huh, Sarge?"

Dixon gave him a swift, startled look, but he didn't comment.

NINE

CARTER'S REMARK was innocently made, just another wise crack. Dixon knew this but he wondered if, in his gross innocence, Carter hadn't come closer to the truth than he realized.

Dixon knew very well that Hagen had spent the night at the chalet. Hagen was quite aware of this, quite aware also of what Dixon could do to stop his romance dead in its tracks if he wished. The Colonel had always been a hard man, a practical man. If anything stood in his way, he removed the obstacle. Fifteen years ago he'd certainly brushed aside the biggest one any man's life could encounter, and done it coldly, with malice and enough careful strategy to get away with it—except with the Department of the Army. They didn't need proof. A suspicion was enough and Hagen had stopped with his rank of full colonel. He should be wearing two stars right now and Dixon had heard when a recommendation for one star had been made, Hagen had been turned down. Plenty of people forgot in time, but the Army never did. And neither had Dixon.

He snapped back to the attention this trip required when his eyes automatically scanned the rear-view mirror and detected a glimpse of sun-reflected glass. A moment later he caught sight of a German motorcycle dispatch rider coming up fast.

"We got company," he told Carter, who whirled around to have a look. In the rear of the truck, the motorcycle had already been seen and Kiley had slipped beneath the canvas, but still covering the POW's and letting them know it.

Carter lifted his BAR. "If he gets curious, Sarge, kinda bend forward so I can shoot behind your head. Okay?"

Dixon nodded. This whole thing was a foul-up. The journey should have been made last night under cover of darkness and to hell with the doubled Kraut patrols. Anybody had a chance in the dark. Here, there was none. An armored car could cut them to pieces, a well-placed road block could machine gun them into ribbons and a tank would have a field day. The Kraut POW's were a lousy stall—they were soldiers, after all, and one of them might feel it worthwhile to die for the Fatherland and yell an alarm.

The motorcycle turned out, put on a burst of speed, rolled on by, and as it passed the staff car, the cyclist waved a greeting. Dixon figured Sal Monda must have aged a couple of years in that last few minutes.

Carter exhaled loudly. "We got away with it."

"One lousy Kraut. Wait'll we hit a roadblock," Carter commented sourly.

Sal Monda's fear showed itself in the increased speed of the staff car. Dixon tramped heavily on the gas pedal and sat hunched over the wheel, trying not to think about Guillaine and Hagen. He'd always had a feeling that some day he'd have to kill him. The urge was stronger in him than ever. He wished he could forget it and concentrate on the job at hand.

Carter broke in on his thoughts. "What gambler's chance do you think we got, Sarge?"

"One in five."

"It's a friggin' mess, ain't it?"

"I wouldn't call it a pushover."

"How're we gonna cross into our lines? That's a Kraut command car up ahead and this goddamn truck is loaded with Krauts in uniform. What'll our patrols think when they see us?"

"We send a radio message. I got the system hooked up to this mike beside me. The problem is, can we get into a position so they can come out and help us. We still got nineteen miles to travel and every mile is gonna get worse."

Carter regarded the countryside that whizzed by him. "Anyway, it beats walkin'."

Suddenly the brake lights on the German staff car blinked and its tires squealed as Monda applied the brakes. Dixon rolled up almost into a crash before the brakes grabbed. Then he saw what had alarmed Monda. Over the brow of the next hill came a Tiger I, a heavy tank with an 88 *kanone* pointed squarely in their direction.

"Jeeze," Carter exclaimed. He twisted around and called a warning to Kiley in back. Carter moved his BAR to cover the German soldiers, let them see the gun and realized he could fan it a couple of times and they'd all be dead. They stared at the muzzle of the weapon in open fear and sat more erect, trying to pose as soldiers on transport.

The tiger was an awesome thing to a tanker whose armor consisted of a medium Sherman. There were bigger tanks, but this one seemed as deadly as a tank could be. If Monda swerved or showed signs of nervousness, the monster was going to stop them. All their machine guns would be as effective as a child's pop gun against that armor.

The German tank commander had his head out of the hatch and he regarded the two approaching vehicles with interest but not with alarm or suspicion. The erect soldiers convinced him everything was as it should be. He didn't even turn his head to look back as the truck passed.

"One more like that and I'm gonna jump," Carter vowed. "And if there's one of them babies on this road, there'll be others."

They were along an isolated stretch of highway. Dixon tapped the horn twice in a signal, and Monda rolled off the road to a stop, with the truck behind him.

Dixon got out and ran to the car. He opened the front passenger door and crammed himself onto the seat, shoving the wounded German over.

"Okay, Sal," he said. "You're doin' fine. Next time I tap my horn once—just once—make an immediate turn off the highway to the right. Cross the fields the best you can, until you're out of sight of the road. Then turn South again and go like hell for our lines. If you see a Yank patrol, stop and get out fast."

"I'm gonna put in for retirement," Sal said in a weak voice. "I'm old enough to be my own grandfather. Didja see that goddamn tank?"

"I saw it. Keep your head now—we've almost got it made. Okay, roll."

Dixon ran back to the truck, started after the staff car, and they covered another eleven miles without an incident. The Germans weren't holding this sector in depth, which was a break.

"How much further?" Carter asked. "I never bothered to look for landmarks on our way in."

"Three miles . . . three lousy miles . . ."

They went into a wide curve and when they straightened out, they saw the roadblock. A Tiger I, a couple of armored cars, motorcycles and troop carriers.

"Mama mia," Carter groaned. "So long!"

Dixon tapped the horn. Monda instantly swerved off the road as directed and the truck followed. Dixon picked up the radio mike and made his call, using the daily code. He repeated it four times before an answer came through. At the same time he was guiding the fast-moving truck over rough ground, sometimes spongy earth, with one hand.

"Blue Fox two miles north of line, moving at thirty with pursuit immediate. Request help. Repeat, request help. We are a Kraut staff car leading one of our cargo carriers."

The message was acknowledged. Carter had listened to Dixon's plan. He chewed thoughtfully for a moment, hanging on grimly, while the truck bounced and tipped.

"We'll make the line in maybe six minutes. How can they get help to us that fast? Hell, they didn't even know we were comin'—and right back of us are the armored cars and the tank. Even the motorcycles are rolling up the road to try and cut us off."

"You take care of them," Dixon said. "I'm bringin' this in if I can."

Four motorcycles bounced off the road ahead of them and moved to intercept. The armored cars were gaining rapidly, but there was still a chance if that damned Tiger didn't start throwing shells.

They heard the flat report a few seconds later and a big chunk of French soil was chewed up by an .88. Dixon couldn't even use evasive tactics. There wasn't time. His only hope lay in the fact that the tank didn't have the range yet, and as the armored cars and motorcycles closed, the gunner would have to stop firing or take the chance of hitting his own people.

Carter casually lifted the BAR out of the truck window, aimed it and the stream of bullets hurled one cyclist off his machine. It kept going a few yards before it bounced, leaped into the air and crashed down. The other three instantly veered off, but one of them didn't make it. Amory in the staff car, cut loose on him with a deadly aim.

Carter twisted around to study the situation behind them. The Tiger was ranging out well into the field, its cannon traversing slowly. The armored cars were going to make a pass and if they failed, the tank gun would try to get them. None of the Germans seemed worried about the fate of the POW's, now crouched down in back, huddled together and trying to find courage in close contact with one another.

"A mile," Dixon breathed. "One gaddamn mile more . . ."

"We ain't gonna make it," Carter said. "They got heavy machine guns in the armored cars trained on us and they're almost in range. I say let's bail out and take our chances."

"The hell we will. There's no profit in that. Where'll you hide? In the hole you'll make when you land?"

"Stinkin' luck," Carter complained. "I said this was a fuggin' mess right from the start."

The two armored cars separated to trap the truck in their cross fire. It wouldn't be long now. Carter saw the planes first—about a dozen of them, coming in low and fast. As they passed over the staff car and the truck, their guns began to hammer the armored cars. Four of them veered off and went after the tank with rockets. It was over in a matter of seconds, and when the planes roared back, the two armored cars were burning, the tank listed to one side and was beginning to smoke, and the two surviving motorcycle troops were roaring back to the highway, having had a belly full.

Carter let out a rebel yell. "We made it! By God, we did it!"

"Yeah," Dixon said unenthusiastically.

"What's eatin' you, Sarge? We're goddamn heroes. Ain't we heroes?"

"I dunno yet. We still gotta go back."

Carter lapsed into silence. Then he shrugged. It was Carter's habit to shrug off things he couldn't

110

control. He'd start worrying on the way back, not now.

Carter thought of something and gave a cackling laugh. "Sarge, is this the way they fought the old war? The First War?"

"Not quite," Dixon said. "Not just like this, Rod."

A dozen tanks burst out of the perimeter to meet them, and they rolled on through to safety and the motor pool where everything was waiting for them. Dixon climbed down off the truck and saluted a Captain who came up on the double.

"We've got wounded and POW's," he reported. "We need two more trucks. Make it three and we'll leave this one. It's kinda beat. All the gas and ammo we can carry—and rations. We'll be set to go as soon as it's dark."

"All right, Sergeant. Take your men to the mess tent. Grab yourself a bite and then report to the Intelligence Officer. We'll take care of your trucks and supplies."

Dixon saluted, but he remained with the truck until the burned and wounded had been transferred to stretchers and were being carried to the field hospital. Then he reported to Intelligence for a two-hour session. It ended with Dixon being given a new map and orders from General Stafford to be delivered to Colonel Hagen.

When Dixon heard those orders, he was half tempted to ask for relief. The brass who thought up this shindig were mad, and Colonel Hagen was even crazier because he'd welcome the chance. The whole thing was worse than this wild trip for supplies.

Dixon got himself a large helping of food and

went over to a tree where he sat down to wait. Half-way through it, his head lolled to one side, he slumped lower and he fell asleep. Nobody bothered him, the sounds of war close by never made him turn a hair. His tin plate of food, resting on his ample stomach, slid down and a gravy-smeared boiled potato rolled off and along his pants, leaving a greasy wake.

As he awoke, the same Captain was walking toward him. Dixon didn't bother to rise and the Captain squatted down beside him.

"Three trucks, best we got. There's enough fuel and ammo, plenty of food, some bazookas and rockets in case you need them. And a supply of plastic explosive. You know how to handle the stuff?"

"I'll handle it." Dixon brushed at the grease stains and wondered how they got on his pants. Someone had removed the food.

"The way we got it figured, the Krauts won't even begin to consider the fact that you'll try to get back and certainly not over the same route you took getting here. But just in case they got ideas you were after supplies, we'll start a diversionary ruckus four miles to the west of your jump-off. We'll even send out some trucks with orders to turn back fast, once the Germans see them. It'll be dark enough in about an hour."

"Okay," Dixon said. "We'll be ready."

He borrowed a razor and shaved, scrounged some fresh clothes and changed into them. He examined his BAR, ran his knife blade over a sharpening wheel and flicked dried blood off it. He had to think a moment where the blood had come from. It seemed a few months ago that the Kraut lieutenant had chased Guillaine across the field and tried to rape her.

It had been yesterday. Dixon wondered why time had a habit of expanding itself in war. He found Carter and Sal Monda drinking beer and judging from the empties, they'd had a ball, though both were sober enough. Dixon went over to the mail truck and turned in the batch of envelopes the Colonel had written to the relatives of those men who had already been killed in this wild tank foray. He discovered Kiley writing a letter.

"Finish it up, soldier," he said. "We are moving out again."

"Okay, Sarge. I was just telling my old man about this. I don't think he'll believe me."

After the censor got through with it, Dixon guessed, all Kiley's old man would do was wonder why the letter had been written, there'd be so little left.

Amory turned up on time. He looked fresh, showered and rested, but he didn't explain to anyone where he'd been. Then Carter appeared. He hadn't bothered to change clothes. Dixon gathered them near the three trucks.

"This time we're loaded and we can't move very fast. We also ride without lights and we don't use the highway. No matter what happens, this stuff has to go through. Keep 'em moving. We take off in twenty minutes."

He walked away and accosted the first Sergeant he met. "I need a bottle or two. Any stuff around?"

"Cognac is all, but it's pretty good."

"It'll do. Where can I find it?"

"Better let me. Cost you six bucks each."

Dixon gave him the money and after he was gone, he wished he'd bought four bottles. The way things were going, he felt he'd very likely need them.

He kept thinking about Gullaine and that brought him around to Hagen. The more Dixon thought about Hagen and this entire operation, the more he believed the Colonel was crazy. It was all a scheme to win himself a lot of glory at the expense of men's lives. If he pulled this off, his old trouble might be forgiven and he'd get his promotion.

When Colonel Hagen became General Hagen, Bert Dixon was going to become a civilian just as fast as he could get the papers. It was bad luck that he and Hagen had come under the same command. Or was it? Could Hagen have arranged this? A bird Colonel wouldn't have much trouble. A word in the right place, a favor asked, and the one man Hagen had reason to fear would be completely at his mercy. In a shooting war, anything can happen. Men die, but at whose hand?

Dixon wanted those bottles very much.

TEN

DIXON DROVE the first truck with Carter seated beside him. Sal Monda was alone in the second and the third carrier was driven by Kiley with Amory riding shotgun. As they moved toward the line, a sudden flare-up of activity occurred about two miles away. Another diversionary move to draw German soldiers to one sector and leave the real crossover point lightly guarded. It worked just as it had the first time.

They were over without trouble, but moving across meadows now, staying off the road until they were deeper into German-held territory. Carter was chewing tobacco again, but the aroma from his mouth wasn't all tobacco. He'd been hitting a bottle before he got aboard, though he was far from drunk. He was, however, talkative.

"You knew the Old Man pretty good before the war, huh?"

"Yeah. I knew him."

"They tell me you even served with him in the first World War. That right?"

"We were there." Dixon remembered very well indeed and some enthusiasm came into his voice. "I guess we had the first damn tank force in United

States history. We borrowed the tanks from the Frogs. Y'know, that was a funny war. Most of the stuff we're using now was developed then. And don't kid yourself, pal. It was as bloody as this one."

"Aw hell, you didn't have the kind of weapons we got."

"What we had were good. And we didn't fight from tanks or fast planes. Somebody blew a whistle and we piled outa trenches and we crossed barbed wire and stacked up our dead on it. We hit the German trenches and we used bayonets. It was a hell of a lot more personal in those days."

"There've been improvements," Carter said. "You die faster now."

"You die maybe, but not faster," Dixon corrected him. "There's heavier firepower today, more destructive power, but you also have better doctors and hospitals and drugs we never heard of then."

"Okay, Sarge, just how would you compare the two wars?"

"There isn't any difference. They're just the same."

Carter cleared a mouthful of saliva overside. "Yeah, I won't argue the point. You never left the army, huh?"

"No. I liked the life and I had a feeling we'd get into another war. This time I wanted to help us be a hell of a lot more effective when we jumped in."

"You worked in tanks all the time?"

"Most of the time. Hagen's an expert with them. He learned how to do things with tanks that were never thought of before."

"Like this fouled-up, friggin' mess?"

"It ain't fouled up, soldier, and we raised plenty

116

hell in one single day. Remember the burning Stukas?"

Carter snorted. "Yeah and I remember the ones that weren't burning as they came down on us. We caught hell too."

"That's the general idea of war, ain't it?"

Carter rubbed his nose with the back of his hand. "I dunno. Me, I never thought much about anything except getting me a job that didn't take much work and paid enough to buy me a bottle and a woman when I wanted them. I didn't think about the next day, because far as I could see, there maybe wouldn't be one. So why should I worry? There's somethin' to that kind of life, Sarge. Not much, but somethin'. But I think I been ruined for it if I ever get outa this stinkin' mess."

"If you want to get out of it alive, stop soundin' off like this and peel your eyes for Krauts. There ain't but about five million of 'em all around us and they're real nasty characters."

"Okay, okay," Carter said. "I think you made a mistake lettin' Monda ride the second truck alone. He's too much a kid. You can't depend on him. All he'll do is start dreamin' of dames. That's all he thinks about."

"He's never been laid," Dixon said. "The kid's virgin."

"Maybe, but I'm tellin' you he won't be if he ever is allowed to sit still where there are dames."

Dixon bent over the wheel, picking out landmarks, hoping they wouldn't wind up in some ravine or have a wheel ripped off by a half-buried rock.

He noted with considerable satisfaction, the two

burned-out armored trucks and the Tiger I, which had been left in the field to rot. And he began to think that Hagen's theory was right—the Krauts wouldn't expect a return over the identical route and therefore, not guard it well.

Dixon wasn't kidding himself about their good luck so far. It could change over the next hillock, around the next bend in the highway which they tried to keep in sight. If they were attacked, there wouldn't be much of a battle. These carriers were crammed with jerry cans of petrol, shells, machine-gun belts, bazooka rockets and high explosives. They'd all go to hell or glory in a split second if a tank found their range.

Sal Monda cursed the fact that they couldn't use lights. It was bad enough driving over these damn fields, but without lights it was murder. Several times he nearly rammed Dixon's truck when he failed to notice it had slowed. And behind him rolled the third truck. If they all piled up, he'd be in the middle. It was enough to make a man think—about women.

Dixon's hunch had been right. Monda had never slept with a woman. His closest experience to sex had happened when he diddled with a fourteen-year-old girl at a block party in his East Side New York neighborhood. Plenty of his contemporaries, even in his fifteen-year-old category, had gone the limit many times and bragged about it. Not that Sal ever had the chance. He'd been a good-looking kid, tall and husky, but somehow he never quite got up the nerve to ask a girl to go the limit with him. Sometimes he wondered if there was anything wrong with him, but he felt grown up now and he knew there wasn't.

He'd seen men killed, though he hadn't killed any-body himself yet—that he knew of. Being a loader wasn't exactly the same as pulling a trigger and he found he could ease his conscience that way.

But he was going to have a woman. Not a kid—a woman—before this was over. Only thing, this outfit hadn't stopped long enough for him to find any. Even that little French village they'd liberated—he'd seen a couple of possibilities there, but he'd never had a chance to even speak to them. It was exasperating as hell, but he'd do something about it soon. Or he'd go nuts. Right off his rocker.

Amory, at the wheel of the third truck, wondered how much longer they'd have to drive over these fields. The road seemed clear, no traffic moved along it. There was darkness to shield them. They could make better time and be back in half an hour from this point, but Dixon stuck to the fields and Amory thought he probably knew what he was doing.

Kiley was contemplatively quiet, thinking of school, bringing into focus again, the picture of the small college with red brick buildings. The kind of a school where a teacher really taught, because he could give pupils individual attention and special help. Amory broke into his dream.

"What's your candid opinion of Sergeant Dixon, Terry?"

"What? Oh . . . okay, I guess. That is, he's not an educated man in the strict sense of the word."

"Except in fighting a war, eh?"

"Yes, I agree he has a liberal education in that field."

"I think we couldn't have drawn a better sergeant,

that's my opinion. The rest of our crew—well, they're fine fellows but . . ."

Kiley laughed. "I know, but you can't hold it against them. Monda's just a kid, a slum kid at that. Carter's a bum, if everything he says about himself is true. But being in a tank is a great leveler, Mike."

"Oh, I agree. The Colonel now . . . if he isn't West Point, he should've been."

"I like working with experts," Kiley commented. "Hagen's one when it comes to tank warfare. I just hope this damned war ends soon. I've got to pick up my life."

"Me too," Amory said. "I want to get married and all I'm afraid of is, we'll finish up here in a few months or maybe a year and then I'll probably pass within a hundred miles of my home town on my way to Japan."

"One way to look at it, if you make it to Japan, you're lucky. We could have been in one of the tanks that got it yesterday."

Amory peered out into the darkness. "I think we're almost there. We'll have to hit the road in a couple of minutes. That forest extends all the way over to this side and there's no road through it."

But it was ten minutes before Dixon made his turn toward the highway. He signaled with brake lights and stopped a hundred yards from the highway. The other two trucks lined up on either side of him. Then shut off motors and sat there in the darkness, just listening.

"Seems quiet," Carter said.

"Yeah—funny thing, we didn't see any traffic on the highway at all."

"Oh hell, they figured all of us were in the truck and the staff car and we got away, that's all there is to it. They're not looking for anybody."

"Think not? What of all the tanks we had? Where'd they go? If you were a Kraut, wouldn't you ask yourself that?"

"Them Stuka pilots probably reported two hits for every one they really got."

"Rod, you're good with a BAR, but you're god-damn stupid in all other ways. The shot-up tanks were counted, down to the last one. I'm afraid there's some kind of a trap set."

"We'd be able to put up one hell of a fight, wouldn't we?"

"Well, we won't know until it happens, so let's find out," Dixon said. He signaled the other trucks to follow him and they rolled toward the highway.

There was a downgrade here, all the way to the narrow dirt road which led into the forest and their hiding place. Dixon got up some speed, cut his motor and let the truck coast. The two trucks behind him caught on to the strategy and did the same, until the three cargo carriers rolled through the night with only the sound of their tires against the pavement and the wind against the hooped canvas covers.

It was necessary to keep braking the heavily-loaded trucks and not allow them to gain too much speed. If the slope had been two percent greater, they'd have had to rely on their low gear, but it was worth the chance of a pileup to gain the silence of a dead motor, especially this close to the turnoff to the forest road.

Things had gone too smoothly. Dixon was suspicious of this kind of luck. The highway should have carried more traffic, or at least a patrol or two. It could be sealed off. Dixon saw something. He hit the brakes.

In the darkness the identity of the tanks was at first hard to distinguish. Besides, Dixon put all his attention to braking to a crawl and then turning left to get off the highway. In some consternation, but no hesitancy, the drivers of the other two trucks did the same. Dixon quickly jumped out of his truck and motioned for silence. Everybody climbed down and joined him.

"Okay! Monda, Kiley . . . Amory . . . you maybe didn't see them, but Carter and I did. There are two tanks parked alongside the highway a hundred and fifty yards this side of our turnoff."

"Krauts?" Sal Monda asked nervously.

"They ain't ours," Dixon said. "I think they're Tigers."

"We're fouled up again," Carter muttered. "Nothin' goes right."

"I'd say everything did," Kiley remarked. "If we hadn't seen them, they could be shelling us right now."

"What'll we do about them?" Amory asked. "Do you think they've got the road blocked off?"

"I think they're sleeping," Dixon said. "I hope so."

"Maybe they spotted the dirt road and decided to hold off until daylight to check on it." Monda suggested.

"Could be," Dixon agreed. "Whatever it is, we sure can't get by them and we can't just sit here and wait, because if anything happens, it'll probably be to us."

"I got me plenty of respect for Tigers," Carter

said. "What'll we do—shoot our pop guns at them?"

"We got something bigger than that," Dixon said. "Bazookas—twenty of 'em, with plenty of rockets."

"Tigers eat 'em up," Carter objected.

"Not at point-blank range."

"We could sure draw a bead," Kiley admitted, "and shoot fast."

"Let's break 'em out," Carter said with the impatience of a killer.

The trucks had been packed by others so they had to search the cargos for the bazookas. Dixon didn't wait for them, but moved further off the highway and made a half circle to come toward the two tanks from the protection of thick brush, extending out from the forest.

They were Tigers, no doubt about that. The main hatches were open, but there wasn't a sound. Dixon moved warily. Some of the tankers might be sleeping just off the highway. He knelt in the darkness and listened for snoring, or heavy breathing, but there were no giveaway sounds.

He crawled back, returned to the trucks. The bazookas were ready. Monda and Kiley carried a supply of rockets. Dixon picked up one of the long, pipe-like weapons.

"I don't make it up there." He pointed the weapon in the direction of the tanks. "They're Tigers all right, a pair of 'em. Hatches open, nobody around. We'll slip up on them and wait."

In single file, they followed Dixon. He led them reasonably close to the tanks and motioned for them to start crawling. They wriggled through the wet grass, making little sound, until they were within deadly range of the two huge monsters sitting there in the dark as if waiting for prey to come by.

Dixon motioned for the others to stay where they were. He left the bazooka and crawled away, moving toward the dirt road. He was riding a hunch, but nothing else made any sense.

He lay prone beside the dirt road, listening again. If his idea was correct, he'd hardly hear any sounds, but there were other ways to determine if anybody had gone down this road. After each use by the Strike Force, the dirt had been swept of all tracks. Therefore, if any vehicle, or any man had slipped down the road, there'd be signs.

Dixon moved out onto the road. It was too dark to see any footprints, but obviously he couldn't remain here until daylight. He had to risk using a light. He carried a lighter and he flicked this on, shielding the flame as much as possible with his cupped hand, while he let feeble light fall upon the dirt.

He found the bootprints in only a minute or two and he didn't wait to check how many. They headed in. None indicated anyone had come out yet. He retreated toward the spot where he'd left his crew.

He lay prone beside Carter, put his lips against his ear. "What I tell you, pass on in a whisper. Way I see it, these two tanks were on search patrol, looking for us. They came to the dirt road after dark and some of the tank crews walked down to investigate. They'll sneak back quietly and radio for more tanks to attack us. We wait here until the Krauts come back. Then we gun them down and bazooka the hell out of the tanks. If it's possible, climb onto them and dump grenades down the hatch. Don't do this if they get to firing their guns, otherwise drop one and close the hatch."

Carter tapped Dixon's arm to show he understood, turned his head and whispered the message to Kiley and this was repeated until each knew the setup.

Dixon left his bazooka on the ground, and indicated Carter was to do the same. They would use their BAR's while Kiley, Amory and Monda would tackle the tanks.

Dixon and Carter crept toward the dirt road. Dixon crossed it, got himself set. With Carter on the other side, they'd turn loose a cross fire on any approaching Germans.

The only thing Dixon dreaded was that the prowling enemy might be spotted by a sentry. If any kind of an alarm was given, the men still in the tanks would promptly slam the hatches closed and either attack or draw off, to radio for help. Either way would be fatal to the Strike Force hidden in the forest.

Then they came. Four of them, moving silently along the road. That meant three more inside each tank, all primed for trouble. At the first shot, the bazookas would attack. With luck, Dixon figured they might make it, but he hated the odds. He'd found it hard to knock out a Tiger with a 75. The bazookas would have to hit exactly right, but then, the bazookas were being fired by tankers who knew precisely where a rocket would do the most damage.

Dixon didn't have to signal Carter. They were set. The four unsuspecting Germans walked, two on either side of the road, ready to dive for cover if anything came up behind them. They were wary, but unworried. Their two big tanks would cover them if anything happened.

Dixon slowly squeezed the trigger, taking the two on the opposite side of the road from where he was positioned, knowing Carter would take care of the others.

He fired a short burst. It was followed by Carter's gun hammering briefly. The four Germans were cut down. There were ten or fifteen seconds of silence and then the bazooka shells slammed home with loud roars and the fire from their explosions lit up the sky.

Dixon and Carter raced along the road to the highway. They saw one man trying to climb out of his tank. Dixon got off a burst, missed. The German dropped down out of sight, but then he reached up to pull the hatch down. Carter kept up a steady fire to discourage him while Dixon raced to the tank.

It was stalled, with one tread dangling, from the effects of the bazooka. Dixon took time to wave his arms in the direction of the tankers turned bazooka men, so they wouldn't fire again. He climbed to the top of the tank, finding it hot to the touch.

He pulled the pin on a grenade, counted slowly, dropped it, took another, pulled the pin and almost lost it in the jar of the first explosion. He dropped the second grenade, jumped off the tank and approached the other one. Nobody had closed this hatch either and there seemed to no signs of life. Suddenly the powerful engines roared to life and the machine-gun turret began to revolve.

Carter was on top of the tank before the gun could swing around to stop him. He pointed his BAR into the hatch and started shooting. The turret stopped moving. Carter dropped grenades inside, slammed the hatch and jumped clear.

After the grenades went off, the engines stopped. There was nothing now but a lot of silence and then Dixon's luck broke. The first tank he'd attacked, suddenly burst into flame. In a minute, ammo would start exploding.

Dixon and Carter set out on a dead run to get away from the vicinity. Dixon didn't stop as he passed Monda, Kiley and Amory. He merely called out, "Get the trucks rolling. Hurry it up."

They backed onto the highway, sped down it to pass the silent tank and the blazing one, made the turn down the road and switched on their headlights as they neared the encampment of Shermans.

The shooting and the explosions had alerted the tankers and they were ready to button up and attack. Dixon jumped off the truck and looked for Hagen. Some men pressed close, wanting an explanation of the shooting.

"There were two Tiger tanks on the highway just beyond this road," Dixon said. "They'd sent men to scout out our position and they must have found it. I don't think they had time to radio a report back."

Lieutenant Miller came running from the vicinity of the jeep. He wore pants, no shoes, but an undershirt and a helmet tightly strapped down.

"Where's the Colonel?" Dixon asked.

"I don't know . . . I haven't seen him . . . been sleeping," Miller said. "What's happened?"

"We may have been spotted, sir. We'd better mount up and get out of here."

"No!" the Lieutenant said.

"Sir . . . the two tanks may have radioed for help, or the fires will be seen."

There were a series of dull explosions from the highway as the tank ammuntion went off and then they saw the glow, even above the tall trees.

"If there are any other Kraut patrols around, they'll see that. We can't stay here."

"We stay, Sergeant, until Colonel Hagen gives the order to move."

"Okay, okay! Where the hell is he?"

"I don't know. I told you, I've been sleeping. . . ."

"Anybody know where the Colonel is?" Dixon asked, and his heart was sinking because he thought he knew exactly where Hagen was.

Somone spoke up from the fringes of the crowd. "He was heading for the village about an hour ago. Some farmer came down to see him. I was on sentry. I passed the farmer through and pretty soon he and the Colonel high-tailed it."

Dixon spoke loudly. "If we can't move, we can get ready for it. Unload the trucks, stow away as much as you can carry. The trucks will roll with us. Assign men to handle them."

"Now hold on," Lieutenant Miller said stubbornly. "I give the orders here."

"Okay—then give them," Dixon shouted. "I told him . . . two Tigers on the highway. There may be a hundred more close by. They'll come here and goddamn it, we don't want to be caught in any trap."

"We will not move until I say so," Miller spoke up loudly. "Unload the trucks, but nobody moves out."

"I'm moving out," Dixon said.

"If you do . . ."

"I'm going to find Colonel Hagen. If you don't like it, shove it, Lieutenant, sir."

Dixon raced back to the truck he'd driven, reached onto the seat and took down one of the bottles of cognac. He opened it, impatient to get at the stuff and tempted to break the neck of the bottle against a tank. He finally pried the cork out, tilted the bottle and took a long drink. He picked up his BAR, slung it over his shoulder and with the bottle in one hand, he began running toward the now fairly well-blazed path to the fields overlooked by the chalet.

ELEVEN

HE STOPPED halfway to the edge of the forest and drank deeply. He had more as he entered the fields and moved along them at a dog trot. He stopped at the chalet gate long enough to set the half-empty bottle on the rubble which the Sherman had made of the cement gateposts. He moved on up the path noisily, not wanting to be shot at by a trigger-happy Colonel who'd resent being rousted out of bed and off his woman in the middle of the night.

Dixon even banged the brass knocker on the door, though it stood ajar. He went in and looked up the stairs. He was very drunk, free of all inhibitions, military or moral.

"Hagen, goddamn your soul, come down here."

"Upstairs, Sergeant." Hagen called back. "Come up here! Stop that damned yelling. And no lights!"

Dixon felt himself getting drunker by the moment. The steps had a tendency to reel slightly and he was forced to cling to the bannister. He thought of the German Major whom Carter had killed with his BAR at the foot of these steps and Dixon burst out laughing at the memory. He had no idea why he should have thought it was funny.

He reached the corridor and weaved his way along it. He paused a moment, closed his lids tightly to clear his vision. When he opened them, he saw the door and made his way to it. It was ajar and he tried to look inside, but the darkness made it impossible.

"You son of a bitch," he said thickly. "If you're in there, speak up!"

"I'm in here," Hagen said quietly.

"Get the hell outa that bed in case I decide to shoot you."

"You're drunk, Sergeant."

"I'm stinking drunk, Just drunk to tell Guillaine what sort of a bastard you are."

"Never mind that now. What about those two Tigers?"

"Tigers? Hell with Tigers. Yeah . . . But I'm one. Boy, am I a Tiger."

"Sergeant, answer me! What about those two German tanks?"

"Just take it easy, Colonel, sir. Nice and easy because if you don't, I'll blow your goddamn lousy guts out."

Guillaine gave a sharp cry of fear.

"Don't you worry, ma'am," Dixon said. "You won't be hurt. Not physically, you won't, but I dunno how you'll feel about this guy when I get through."

Hagen didn't move. He couldn't tell for sure in the dark, but he suspected Dixon's BAR was poised and ready.

Dixon went on. "I'm gonna tell you about our great Colonel, ma'am. Looks to me like you been a pushover for him, so you oughta know just what kind of a rat he is. And I hope you understand everything I'm telling you because I can't speak French. So if you don't get the drift, just stop me. Okay?"

Hagen said, "Bert, this time you're going too far. Not because I am afraid of what you're going to say, but we happen to be in a war. . . ."

"We always been in one, Colonel," Dixon said. "Yes sir, we never did get outa the First World War and this is our Third World War. The second one was between ourselves. Ma'am, you ever know the Colonel was married?"

Oui," she said. "I know."

"Let him talk," Hagen said. "It's been tying him up in knots for fifteen years. Let him get it off his chest and then we can go back to fighting the war."

"Y'know," Dixon said sarcastically, "he's bluffin'. He figures if he acts like this . . . you know . . . what the hell . . . that sorta thing, then he thinks what I got to say won't mean so much. Won't sound so bad. But lemme tell you this, ma'am. There just ain't any way to soften murder."

Guillaine moved closer to the Colonel and gripped his hand tightly.

Hagen said, "Bert, she's standing beside me. Be careful with that gun. If you got any ideas about using it, give her a chance to get out of here."

"Just stay put," Dixon said. "Both of you. If I decide to kill you, Colonel, I'll give her a lot of time to move away. I don't want to kill her. I coulda been in love with her . . . but you hadda horn in. Like you always did. But you don't get her, Colonel. No part of her, even if the two of you have been in bed." He laughed loudly. "Are you dressed, Colonel? You got your pants on? Now that'd be funny, if they found the Colonel here dead, with his pants off."

"Bert, if you have to talk, go ahead, but get it over with because if you don't, you'll have to kill me to stop me from killing you."

Dixon sobered. "Listen to him. You think he's a big, brave man, huh? You'd never guess he's a woman killer now, would you? Okay, so lemme tell you what happened. The Colonel and me . . . we came outa the first war okay and we stayed in the army. We got married. His wife's name was Alicia, a real doll, but not like you. She didn't have your class, what I mean, but a doll anyhow. My wife was Lois . . . she she was a doll too. You never saw a girl with such nice hair and such blue eyes and . . . everything . . ."

"Let's concede our wives were beautiful women," Hagen said tartly.

"Take it easy," Dixon said angrily. "I ain't in a hurry and you shouldn't be."

"Please, Sergeant Dixon," Guillaine implored, "either finish what you have to say or let us go."

"All in good time. Maybe you want me to turn on a light, huh? So I can see both of you. I'll lay odds neither of you got a stitch on. Y'know, Colonel, this is a hell of a way to fight a war—in bed."

"Damn you," Hagen said softly.

"Okay . . . I'll finish it up. You listenin', ma'am?"

"Yes," she answered in a whisper.

"Well, the Colonel here, he didn't get along with Alicia. They fought all the time. I know because my Lois and the Colonel's lady were friendly. Real buddies and Alicia told Lois all about it. This bum you've been sleeping with, used to beat her up. He cursed her and beat her until she couldn't take any more and she decided to leave him. Lois . . . that was my wife, remember?—she helped Alicia pack and she was driving her to a railroad station. We were in California then . . . runnin' our tanks all over the mountains and the desert."

"Guillaine," Hagen said, "let me finish for him. . . ."

"Oh no," Dixon's voice crackled. "This is my story. I'm tellin' it my way. Lois was drivin' Alicia, but the Colonel here, heard about it and went after them in his car. He caught up with them on a mountain road and he drove them over the side of a cliff. The skid marks, the brake marks, everything showed that's what he did. He killed them both. The son of a bitch wasn't content to kill his own wife, he had to kill mine too."

"I do not believe it," Guillaine said promptly and firmly.

"Ask him. Go ahead—one thing he never was, is a liar. Ask him! Also ask why he's still a Colonel and been one for more'n twenty years. Ask him why he gets passed over time after time when they're lookin' for a new general. Ask why he didn't get a star on this operation. I'll tell you. He wanted it, they asked for it, but the War Department turned him down, because while they didn't have enough on him for a court-martial or even a civilian trial for murder; they know what he did and they don't want any generals who are murderers."

"It's true, about my being passed over," Hagen said. "The reason is also true. What happened that night has been entered against my record."

"Then you did kill the two women?" Guillaine asked.

"Sergeant Dixon says I did. Sergeant Dixon insists all the evidence shows I did. The law doesn't say so, neither do the military authorities who investigated."

"If it ain't true, why didn't you stand up and prove it? Goddamn you, by remaining silent you admitted your guilt and I oughta blast you good, Colonel."

"Guillaine," Hagen said, "Please move to the other side of the room. This fool may decide to shoot when I light this lamp."

"I will remain with you, Luke."

"No—do as I say, I haven't time to argue with this lunatic and in his present condition there's no telling what he might do."

Guillaine moved. Dixon could hear her. He braced himself. Hagen was up to something. Then a match flared, was transferred to an oil lamp wick and yellow light filled the room. Dixon saw that Hagen was fully dressed. There were field glasses hanging around his neck. He wore a side arm, with the flap down. Guillaine too, was fully dressed.

"Now I'm going to say something," Hagen told Dixon. "Just once. I came here because a farmer ran to our camp and told me German tanks were in the neighborhood. From the windows of this chalet, you can study the countryside and a while ago there was enough starlight to see a tank by. I watched those Tigers pull out of town and I've been watching to see if any more showed up. Now, what happened to those tanks?"

"We blasted them," Dixon said. "Me and my crew. We killed the crews."

"And set fire to the tanks so every German within sight will see the fires."

"Go to hell," Dixon retorted. "We did what hadda be done. I didn't see you around to give the orders."

"Why didn't you pull our tanks out? You did bring ammo and gas back, I hope."

"Three carriers of everything we need. More'n we need, but we didn't pull out because Lieutenant Miller turned yellow. He won't move unless you tell him to and he knew damn well you were busy up here . . ."

"Sergeant," Guillaine said, "we have been watching through the windows for a long time. That is all."

"Okay . . . okay, I was wrong there. But I ain't wrong about the overall picture and I hope to hell I queered you tonight, Colonel. I hope you fell in love with this wonderful woman and now you'll lose her like I lost Lois. I been waitin' to square that for a long time."

"Do you consider it squared then?"

"It'll do until another time."

Hagen lifted the binoculars from around his neck and placed them on a small table beside him. He walked casually toward Dixon.

"If you're going to pull that trigger, Bert, you'd better start now because I'm going to break your silly face."

"Hold it." The BAR, aimed at Hagen, didn't waver. "Don't go nuts, Colonel. I don't care if I kill you."

"I'm sure of it, but you're too much an army man to kill a Colonel. And it's a Colonel coming at you now, Bert, not a man named Luke Hagen. Put down that BAR."

"You ain't got the guts to move in on me while I hold this gun on you," Dixon said.

Hagen moved briskly toward him. Dixon backed away two steps, hesitated, backed up two more, but the gun remained steady.

"A man who's going to shoot doesn't threaten, doesn't talk it over, doesn't back away. He shoots!"

Dixon snapped on the safety and threw the gun into the corner. "I don't need a gun with you, sir."

"All right if you want it this way, but the Colonel just stepped out of the picture and it's Luke Hagen you're going to swing at, Bert."

Dixon gave a savage cry and leaped. But his reflexes were slow, his mind too befuddled with alcohol. He ran straight into a hard jab that caught him just under the heart, driving all the air out of his lungs and making him cry out in pain. He half turned away from the force of the blow. A strong hand gripped his arm, yanked him back and Hagen hit him on the point of the jaw. Dixon flew back, hit the wall and slid down to a sitting position.

Hagen turned to Guillaine. "I'm sorry, darling. I had to do this before the idiot got himself in real trouble. And I've got to run. I'll be back. I promise you I'll come back if you want me."

She moved up to him and kissed him firmly on the lips. "I want you to come back to me. What I have heard is too silly to be considered."

"There's an answer," Hagen said. "I'll tell it to you as soon as I can."

"What will you do to him?"

"Nothing. It's not his fault. I'm going to lug him back and get my tanks rolling."

"Yes . . . and don't hate this man, Luke."

"I never have and I never will. Good-bye, Guillaine."

He hoisted Dixon over one shoulder. Guillaine picked up the BAR and helped Hagen sling it over his other shoulder. Then he carried Dixon down the stairs and on out of the house. Halfway across the fields, Dixon began to move and mutter in Hagen's ear. By the time they were at the fringe of the forest, Dixon was demanding to be put down.

Hagen set him on his feet, grasped him by the front of his uniform and shook him hard.

"What happened back there is nobody's business. Not even ours, while this emergency is on. Do you understand that, you drunken slob?"

"Okay . . . okay . . . lemme go. I can't breathe . . ."

"You came very close to not having any need for it," Hagen said. "I hope you got all this off your mind now because your mind had better be damned good and clear. Did you bring back orders?"

"Yes . . . they're in the truck I drove."

"Do you know what they read?"

"I know some of it."

"Then you realize we've got a job ahead of us. We've proven the tanks as a strike force already. Now let's wrap it up with a big ribbon. Can you walk?"

"I'm okay, I said."

"We'll settle this later. No time now."

He gave Dixon a hard shove that sent the sergeant stumbling ahead of him. They made quick time along the forest path and found a restless and nervous group of tankers wondering what they should do next.

Leiutenant Miller got out of the jeep and saluted. "We've been waiting for you, sir," he said.

"Why didn't you move out?" Hagen asked angrily.

"Not without your permission, sir."

"Lieutenant, I wouldn't trust you to make your way back to our lines alone and I'm damned if I'll spare a man to wet-nurse you on the way. You'll have to come with us, but I'm telling you right now, if I hear you give one command, I'll shoot you. Now get on one of those trucks and stay there."

He walked rapidly to where the three now-half-emptied trucks stood. From the seat of the first one, he took the orders which Dixon had carried. He ripped the seal, held the papers under a dash light of the truck and read them.

He walked around to the back of the truck and hauled himself onto the tailboard.

"Attention. Everybody . . . move up. You all have to hear this. It's important." He waited a few moments while they gathered closer. "As you know, we're an experimental force. If we prove we can successfully operate with tanks behind enemy lines, stronger forces will be sent out. Many of them, to cut the Germans to pieces. So far, we've done very well, but now we have a new objective. We move from here a hundred and fifteen miles deeper into France—until we hit the Rhine."

"Keerist!" someone said. "Are we goin' into Germany?"

"Exactly. German soil hasn't been invaded as yet. The Germans—Hitler and the others—say it can't be done. They swear no force on earth is strong enough to enter the Fatherland, so we're going to show them how wrong they are. We do this quietly, so we can get out again. It's no suicide mission. First there's a bridge. We take it, hold it, move over it for a foray against a certain German city. It's important militarily for reasons you'll learn later. We take that city apart with tanks. They did it in Poland, Czechoslovakia, Holland, Belgium and France and the German people yelled 'Heil Hitler' when their tanks blasted civilians as well as soldiers. We're going to show them how it feels. How does that sound? And don't yell. Just wave your hands if you want to show how you feel about it."

The silent cheer indicated that no one objected, no one wanted to crawl out. Hagen next made a quick check of the gas and ammo supply, of the food situation. Dixon stood by, now and then touching his slightly swollen jaw. Hagen paid no attention to him.

The Colonel climbed aboard his jeep, started the motor and then twisted around in the seat. His men were mounted up, commanders in the open hatches. Camouflage had been stowed away.

"Sergeant Dixon," Hagen called out.

Dixon moved up on the double.

"Your tank is to hook onto the two Tigers you knocked out and drag them into the woods. Try to obliterate all trace of them if you can. Clean up this area, brush out tread tracks and gather up any loose ends. If the Germans find this place, make them wonder if there were any tanks here."

"But Colonel . . . you'll be moving out without us . . ."

"I think I made my orders clear. You've studied the map. You know the route. We'll travel the Norman Road for the first thirty-two miles. We travel only by night. Find us, catch up with us, but do this job first."

"Yes, sir," Dixon saluted. "Sir . . . I just want you to know . . ."

"I haven't time to listen, Sergeant. All you have to do is what you've been told."

Hagen raised his arm and swept it forward as he began moving the jeep. The tanks fell in line, the trucks followed up and Dixon and his tank were left alone in a matter of a few minutes.

Dixon climbed onto *Daisy*. All hatches were open. He didn't need the tank communication system.

"We drag the two Tigers out of sight. We come back here and police the area, then we catch up."

"Hell, they'll have too much of a start," Monda complained.

"They're goin' all the way to Germany, ain't they? Gives us time. Now get with it."

140

TWELVE

SEVENTEEN MEDIUM Sherman tanks, three trucks and a jeep, moving in single file through darkness, charting their devious route by compass, starlight and broad guessing, but nobody doubted they were headed straight for their target.

Before dawn, Dixon's tank caught up with the line after rolling at high speed along a cement road, through countryside so peaceful they sometimes wondered if there was a war going on.

Dixon ate the dust of the other vehicles and his helmeted, goggled face soon was black with dirt. When he raised the goggles, he looked as if he were wearing a white mask.

Without question, this operation had been set up with the help of the French Free Forces, because no American patrols could have penetrated this far. They would spend two nights on their journey to the Rhine, traveling only in darkness and often at reduced speeds but the steady grind would consume the miles.

The two stops where they would hide and rest, had been prepared. The first night they spent in a forest, just like the one they'd left. Before dawn, the tanks were camouflaged again, the men slept, shaved, washed up as best they could. Tanks were refueled, guns were cleaned and polished.

Hagen slept in one of the trucks. Lieutenant Miller was now driving another of them, relieving a real tank man for work inside a Sherman, where he belonged.

Dixon's jaw was sorer than ever. He had trouble eating, but the cognac slid down smoothly, though he was very careful not to drink enough to show it.

He had a vague feeling something was wrong. Not with the action he was engaged in, but with his dealing with Hagen on the personal side. For fifteen years he'd waited to tell the truth about Hagen, but it didn't seem to have gone over. Even he himself, wasn't satisfied with the way he'd done it, or with the result. Hagen so far seemed unaffected by it and Guillaine hadn't walked out of his life.

But she'd most certainly walked out of Sergeant Bert Dixon's. He berated himself half the night, but before dawn he'd all but forgotten the incident while he concentrated on ways and means of protecting the rear of the tank column.

By the second night he was fighting the war again, but he noticed that, as before, Hagen left him on the tail to eat more dirt. Dixon gave vent to some army anger at this, to which his crew cheerfully subscribed, but there wasn't much they could do about it. The second night they entered an isolated French village and, by prearrangement, met half a dozen Free French.

Everything was done with great dispatch and Dixon soon acquired a great admiration for the way this had been planned and executed.

For each tank and truck, there was a barn ready to receive them. Whatever the barn contained, had been carefully moved out of the way. Livestock was doubled up. Men with rakes covered the tracks of the tanks and that night the tankers ate a hot meal of chicken stew, prepared by the farm wives.

Colonel Hagen spent half the night going from one barn to another, talking to the crews. He frankly admitted they were bound to suffer more losses, but what they'd accomplish would be of a very special and important nature.

Now that they were close to the bridge and the small town three miles the other side of it, he could tell his men that this town was noted for one thing—the assembly of the V-2 flying bombs being used against England, and now manufactured in quantities to be used against Allied troops when they moved into Germany.

The town was named Dressel. It was strategically located for the final assembly of the rockets and here the experts put them together for quick shipment to the launchers located closer to the channel.

Hagen made certain that every man understood how important their mission was. The only man who seemed unaffected by the magnitude of the attack was Lieutenant Miller, who merely listened with a blank expression on his face.

Hagen was without officers and that was a serious condition. Dixon was as good as two lieutenants, but so far he'd refrained from using him. Dixon had eaten dirt and dust for two days and even that didn't seem punishment enough. However, in the face of his great need for the man, Hagen sent for him.

Dixon entered the barn where Hagen made his headquarters. It contained only the jeep and the folding table and chairs which traveled with Hagen. His maps were spread out for planning the final thrust which would come in the morning, and the area near the table was illuminated by an electric lantern.

Dixon saluted smartly and stood at attention. Hagen looked up at him without much enthusiasm.

"Oh, sit down," he said irritably. "You never made it a point to be respectful around me when we were alone. Don't start now."

Dixon sat down stiffly. "Yes, sir," he said.

"Whatever's between us, Sergeant, will be put to one side until this is over. Do you understand?"

"Yes sir. I wanted to tell you this before, but you wouldn't stand still . . ."

"It's agreed, then. It's also obvious I can't use Lieutenant Miller, so you're second in command. I like the way you handled the two Tigers checking on us back there. It was no good to tell you so at the time, but I do now. It was done well enough to win you gold bars. A battlefield promotion. How about it?"

"No sir. I don't want it."

"I could make you accept, you know."

"You could make me wear 'em, but you couldn't make me feel like a lieutenant, sir. I want to stay just where I am."

"All right, but if anything happens to me, you take over. I assume you'll do that much."

"I'll take over, sir."

"Very well. Now listen carefully. In the morning we begin operating in daylight. There are no heavy German forces anywhere about, except in Dressel

144

which we'll attack. There may be enough of them here to give us trouble. Now we have a bridge to cross. It has to be taken. Look at the map . . . this point . . ."

Dixon studied the map and the river it spanned. The Rhine was at one of its narrowest points here, but still that wasn't going to be an easy crossing, because the bridge was bound to be defended.

"I could take a few men, sir, and swim the river," Dixon said hopefully. "We could maybe take the bridge guards on the other side before they knew what happened."

"And before they could pick up a phone and give an alarm," Hagen added emphatically.

"We'd cut the wires first. At positions as far back from the front as this, the Krauts wouldn't be apt to bury or hide the phone wires. They'll be strung on trees, poles, anything."

"Will one crew be able to handle it?"

"Depends on how many men are guarding the bridge, sir."

"The French tell me they've scouted the area and usually about ten Germans are on duty on each side."

"One crew will be fine. My own crew."

"We'll have to leave a tank to cover the bridge until we get back to mine it completely. You leave your tank on this side. After we're across, you will arrange to take over one of the other tanks. The crew you replace will plant the explosives on the bridge, guard the approaches to it and wait until we return. If we don't get back, they're to blow the bridge and move out with the trucks."

"Yes sir."

"Once we start to roll, it will be at top speed and straight to this town. We'll start shelling it as we move in and before we leave, the factories and the ammo dumps will all be blown sky-high—or we don't leave."

"Think we'll make it, sir?"

"I don't know. Some of us won't. Once we pull out of the town and head back, the Germans will soon know about the attack and they'll send everything they have at us. We're a hundred and fifty odd miles from our lines. True, the territory we retreat over is not heavily manned, because the Germans have been sending too many reinforcements to stop Monty. But they also know Patton is ready to jump off, and they're a damned sight more scared of him than they are of Monty. That means they'll be prepared to move against us as fast as if we were Patton's Lucky Forward."

"We can do a hundred and fifty miles in a day if we're fueled up and we can use the highways."

"We'll have the gas all right, but they'll cover the roads first. They'll have search planes up and once we're spotted, the Stukas will come and the Panzers and Tigers. Everything they have close enough to move quickly. But this is my idea, Sergeant. You had a hand in it too. We used to make it work in mock warfare, though we did get theoretically clobbered a few times."

"I remember. Not trying to horn in on your plans, but the scatter effect might be the best to use. After we cross the bridge again, everybody for himself."

"I've given that some thought, but I've decided against it. As a unit we still pack a lot of authority

146

ut if we're attacked by a superior force, then we
catter. If that happens, we're going to lose heavily."

"How else do you fight a war, sir? We'll do a thou-
and times more damage than we're worth."

"If the men agree with that, we're in."

"They do. I've sounded 'em out. They're polite to
ou, but they talk straight to me. They may gripe and
eef, but they're in this to the finish."

"Do you believe they realize the importance of this?
t's not just destroying a bridge so the Germans will
e impeded bringing up supplies after Patton jumps
ff. It's not the destruction of the place where they
ssemble the V-2 bombs. The real damage will be
sychological. When Patton moves, the German sol-
iers will have heard of this exploit of ours, and
hey'll wonder how they're expected to win the war
vhen we can get behind their lines and do all this
amage before we're stopped. They'll get the nervous
hought that the Third Reich isn't as invulnerable as
hey've been taught and maybe Hitler is a little crazy
or carrying on the war. It's a blow to morale, Bert,
nd that does more damage than bullets."

"Shock the hell out of them," Dixon agreed. "How
ar do we go with reference to the civilians in Dres-
el?"

"This is a city which can't be thought of except as
 military target. The Nazis didn't worry about that
n any of their advances, but if we have men who do,
hen assure them it's actually a military objective and
nyone there has to be considered as military person-
el. We're going to level the town if we can."

"You won't impress the Krauts any other way,"
Dixon said. "I'm all for it. I've seen too many towns

they blasted, and I've heard too many stories of thei
damned POW camps and the extermination centers.
lost my scruples some time back."

"Very well. Get yourself some rest. We move ou
just before daylight to get the element of surprise or
our side. You will jump off first and try to be acros
the river ready to attack by the time we roll up. Tha
will be exactly 0530 hours. Good luck, Bert."

Dixon nodded and went out without saluting
Hagen promptly turned off the lantern, rolled himsel
in a blanket and went to sleep.

Dixon felt no need for rest. He was keyed up with
the coming action and his part in it. He woke up hi
crew and assembled them beside the tank. Kiley wa
sneezing every few minutes and blamed it on an al
lergy for hay.

"You'll soon be outside," Dixon told him and the
others. "We've got a special part in tomorrow morn
ing's work."

"Another one?" Carter groaned. "Do we alway
get the easy stuff?"

"This won't be hard unless you call swimming the
Rhine, killing the outpost on the other side of the
bridge, hard work."

Amory whistled out loud. "Now that ought to be
interesting. Maybe we better find out if we all car
swim."

It seemed they could and nobody was backing
down, though Sal Monda wasn't growing hoarse with
cheering. However, he looked more interested when
Dixon outlined the rest of the plans.

"The tanks will move over the bridge, one crew
will stay behind to guard it and mine it. We rol

traight to this town and blast it. I mean we burn it
ut. Then we head back, cross over the river and the
ridge will then be blown up. We got a hundred and
fty miles to cover before we reach home. It can be
one."

"I figured day before yesterday was about as lousy
s a day could be," Carter griped. "We only had
hirty miles to go that day. No—sixty, because like a
unch of pissed-off screwballs, we had to travel thirty
iles back again."

"What's a hundred and fifty miles," Monda said
vith weak humor, "long as we don't hafta walk it."

Dixon said, "Do you guys need sleep, or shall we
et started and have that bridge ready to take nice
nd early?"

"I like swimmin' in the dark," Carter said.

"We might get fouled up," Kiley agreed, "and need
nore time. I think it's a good idea to get started
ow."

"Sure," Amory said. "This time of night the Krauts
vill be off guard and maybe half asleep. By dawn
hey may be more awake. This is the best time."

"Okay. I'll tell the Colonel we'll leave our tank
ere. We got a mile hike to the bridge. We carry
3AR's, side arms, grenades."

"I'm takin' a bazooka," Carter insisted. "The
ridges are mostly guarded by anti-aircraft guns and
hey could raise hell if they got a bead on any of our
anks."

"You won't find it easy to swim with one of those
ogging you down, Rod," Dixon warned.

"I'm a human fish. Nothin' weighs me down that I

want to carry. Someone has to pack a few rockets, though."

They agreed to carry all they could. Dixon returned to the Colonel's barn and woke him up.

"Me and my crew are pulling out now, sir. Just in case we might be delayed. Gives us plenty of time."

"As you wish. The same jump-off hours goes for the rest of us."

"We'll be waiting."

Dixon armed himself well and led the crew to the farm road and along it. They walked in silence and were ready to dive for cover because Germans could be moving about this area. They were in unfamiliar territory besides, and had to proceed slowly. The Germans often had a habit of setting up a guard post at a most unlikely place, and if they stumbled on one of those, that would be the end of the foray.

Luck held. There were no guard posts, nothing all the way to the river and there they studied the situation through night glasses.

"Two ack-ack guns on this side, two on the other," Dixon said softly. "It's a long bridge, a wide river. Wider than I figured from the map. Sal, you got wire cutters?"

"Yeah . . . sure. . . ." Sal Monda produced them.

"Okay. This is the deal. Sal stays here until fifteen minutes before our tanks roll up. The rest of us swim over now. We locate the telephone wires on the other side. At five minutes before 0630, we cut the wires. Sal, you cut them on this side. Cut them several times, take out whole sections. Then swim over and join us. You'll be in time to celebrate dawn with fireworks."

"Okay, Sarge," Sal said, pleased with the fact that he'd been delegated to an important role. "I'll be all set."

"Let's go," Dixon said, and they crept forward quietly now, their hearts beginning to pound with excitement and sometimes their blood ran cold, wondering what their prospects were for getting out of this.

Sal dropped back, the others reached the edge of the river. They could see a pair of sentries, one on each side of the bridge, pacing their posts slowly. One by one the men slipped into the water, Carter trying to hold the bazooka clear, but failing most of the time. Carter was the strongest swimmer and reached shore first. He offered a hand to help Dixon and the others out as they reached the other side.

It was cold, they were dripping wet and uncomfortable as they made their way to a clump of bushes where they found refuge for a time.

Nobody spoke. They removed some of their wet clothes and spread them in the hopes they'd at least partially dry. They turned their attention to their weapons after that, drying them, making certain they were in perfect order. Carter fussed with the bazooka long after the others lay down on their backs to stare at the sky and get a little rest.

Carter finally joined them and promptly emitted a snore that got him a foot in the ribs. Dixon sat up.

"Stay awake," he told Carter. "You snore."

"I never snore," Carter protested. "Nobody ever told me before I snore."

151

"You do now. Keep your eyes open and your mouth shut."

"How much more time?"

"Less than an hour."

"I could sure use a few minutes sleep."

"I'll gag you if you try it." Dixon decided to keep Carter's mind occupied. "How do you think Sal will make out all by himself?"

"He'll do okay."

"Does he still have women on his mind?"

"Nothin' else but women. If we ever get back to some city that's got a whorehouse, I'm gonna blow him to his first piece. I'll pay for five more if he'll let me watch the first time."

"Sometimes I think you're as green as the kid."

"Me?" Carter said too loudly. He dropped his voice. "You know better'n that, Sarge. Hell, I left 'em spread-legged from here to Spokane. Y'know, I think the Colonel's been layin' that French broad. The one who lives at the chalet."

"You do, eh?"

"I also think you caught them at it. The night before we moved out. He was up there and last I saw, you were luggin' a bottle and gettin' plastered on your way to the same place."

"I went there."

"Find 'em in bed?" Carter asked lecherously.

"I found the Colonel checking the village and the road with field glasses. He'd been tipped those two Kraut tanks were around and he was giving up his sleep to observe."

"No kiddin'. I'd have sworn he was beddin' down

with her. Not that I blame him. And I also figured you were thinkin' about the same thing."

"Maybe—before I got to know her. She don't bed down, Rod. Not willingly. The Krauts raped her a couple of times, I think. She hinted about that. Makes me goddamn happy that I'm going to bust up one of their towns in a little while."

"What we oughta do is take a few of them *frauleins*," Carter smacked his lips. "I heard they're pretty nice."

"You'll be too busy to think of *frauleins*," Dixon told him. "But if you get the urge anyway, don't do it."

"What time now?"

"We got a few more minutes. Go on, close your eyes. If you snore, I'll boot you one."

Carter settled down. "Thanks, pal. I still say I don't snore. I never have. Funny thing . . . never in my life."

His snores, a few seconds later, were too low to be heard. Dixon let him sleep. He sat there thinking about dawn and what would happen during the new day. There was going to be hell to pay in that town and more hell after they left it and tried to make their lines. It seemed an absolutely impossible venture.

Dixon hummed softly, looked at his watch and then closed his own eyes for the few remaining moments.

THIRTEEN

FOUR MEN against ten as dawn began to sparkle against the dewy grass. There'd be five in a few minutes, when Sal Monda finished his swim across the river. Dixon had seen him slip into the water, which meant communications on the other side of the bridge were out.

Carter had already severed the wires on this side. Dixon's watch told him the tanks would come barreling down the road to the bridge in less than four minutes.

The garrison buildings were all on this side and consisted of a barracks building, a supply depot probably full of ack-ack shells and a chemical toilet outhouse.

"All the comforts of home," Carter whispered to Dixon. "I hope one of the Krauts is on the pot when we cut loose. I'd like to see him make time with his pants down."

"You aim that bazooka at the AAA guns. Take the one on your left first, while I keep the men away from the other one. Then put a rocket into the second. Okay?"

Carter propped the cumbersome weapon on his

shoulder and sighted it. Kiley stood by to load, while Amory aimed his automatic rifle on the door of the barracks building. The sleeping Germans would come out that way. With luck, Dixon figured they could have this over with in two or three minutes. According to the map, the town they intended to attack was too far away for all this shooting to be heard.

He was listening for the tanks. The early morning was very quiet. The sentries on the bridge were moving slowly, unsuspicious of the death that was going to cut loose around them in a moment. And why not? They were more than a hundred and fifty miles from enemy forces.

Dixon heard the tanks about the same time the sentries did, but they showed no particular alarm. This was too deep in German territory. This was, in fact, Germany. The Third Reich was invulnerable—Hitler said so—and that had been drilled into the sentries. They merely waited to see how many German tanks started rolling down the road toward the bridge.

The first of the line appeared, topped the ridge and headed down at top speed. Dixon said, "Fire!"

The bazooka shot its rocket at the first gun emplacement, was reloaded immediately and a second rocket followed the first. The men on duty at the gun never knew what hit them. Dixon was firing at the squad in charge of the second gun. They were frantically trying to lower the weapon for level shooting at the line of tanks. They got it about halfway down when Dixon's hail of steel took effect. The men who weren't cut down, dived for cover and then the bazooka hit. When the smoke died away, one gun was tipped at an impossible angle, the other was a blackened ruin.

Amory's rifle caught the sleepy Germans as they came out of the barracks. Dixon scrambled to his feet and ran toward the building as Amory stopped shooting. Kiley joined him and Amory fanned out to the left to give them cover. Carter stayed with the loaded bazooka, looking for a target.

On the other side of the river, the first tanks had knocked over the AAA guns with their first barrage and now their machine guns were mopping up the men who had escaped. The sentries on the bridge were securely trapped. There was nowhere to go. One of them threw his rifle overside and raised his arms as high as he could get them. The other promptly did the same.

Dixon reached the barracks door. Everything had quieted down now, but there might be Germans inside. He poked his rifle around the corner of the door, gave a leap across the entrance as he pulled the trigger.

Someone fired at him. Then there was a scream, followed by sudden silence. Dixon cautiously entered the building, stepping over dead Germans to do it. There was no one left. The man who'd shot at him had been caught squarely in Dixon's burst.

He checked the victims of Amory's deadly fire and found they were either dead or dying. He saw Sal Monda coming up at a run, swearing fluently because he'd been too late to get in on any of the shooting. Dixon looked around with grim satisfaction.

The tanks were moving across the bridge. The

crew of the last one stopped and climbed out to take over guard duty and demolition work.

Immediately two of these men began to attach the plastic explosives to the bridge, working their way across. The two sentries were prisoners, sitting disconsolately on the side of the road with their hands clasped behind the back of their necks.

Colonel Hagen was riding the first tank, his head and shoulders visible above the turret. He saw Dixon, waved and got an okay signal in return. The tanks rolled on while Dixon and his men hurried to the one which had been turned over to them.

Rod Carter slipped into his seat, prepared to roll her out. Amory checked the 75 and Sal Monda made certain he had a full supply of shells. Kiley manned the bow gun and Dixon sat in the turret. He strapped the intercom mike to his throat.

"Let's go," he said.

The Sherman moved out, quickly catching up with the others. It would be the last in line, but Dixon knew there'd be action for all of them. Maybe too much.

Colonel Hagen waited until his lead tank made a lumbering turn at the last curve in the road. Now it led straight down to the town. From his position, it looked like a sleepy little place, except that it had a very large freight siding. Just beyond the limits, on the other side of the town, were long gray sheds where the bombs were assembled. So far, no alarm seemed to have been given. Hagen slid down, closed the hatch over his head and picked up the network microphone.

"Blue Fox One to all commanders, prepare to attack."

The approaches to the town were wide open. Apparently in days of peace it had been an agricultural center and beside the road were wide open fields. For tank maneuver, nothing could have been any better. Under Hagen's crisp orders, the tanks began to fan out. Their speed on the road had been thirty-five miles an hour and this was cut by ten to fifteen miles when they hit the fields, but they were close enough now.

Hagen watched through his periscope. The rooftops of the houses were almost close enough to throw a stone at. They were gray shingled for the most part, a few were thatched. There were nicely kept yards, just as in any small community back home. He could see military trucks moving along the streets and a few people were already abroad, but so far nobody had considered these tanks as any except their own. Certainly they must have been seen and heard.

They were moving in as close as possible. Drivers were seeking streets that cut through the town. Hagen was aiming for the wide Main Street which ended where the gray factory buildings were located.

He turned to the network radio. "Blue Fox One—all commanders—open fire!"

Hagen's tank got off the first round, an A-P shell that blew up the cottage in Amory's sights and all but demolished the ones on either side of it.

Sixteen tanks cut loose, firing as fast as the guns could be loaded. Sal Monda felt the sweat pour down his face and the acrid smell of the gun gases produced a violent headache, which they always had with him, but he'd never mentioned it and he wasn't going to now. Empty shells crashed to the floor of the tank after each shot. Monda rammed in the next shell and slammed the breech block one second before Amory fired. They were using H-E and A-P shells alternately.

The south end of the town was afire. People milled about, helpless, scared, desperate. The machine guns were aimed at the houses, not the people, but some of them died anyway. Two fat dead horses were stretched across the street, and Carter cursed as he rolled the tank onto the sidewalk and brought down a telegraph pole as he avoided the animals.

Hagen's voice came over the intercom. "Bow gunner . . . soldiers coming out of the Inn."

Kiley's 50 mm machine gun rotated toward the little hotel, cut loose and the German soldiers either dropped or scurried back to safety.

"The Inn is probably the CP," Dixon said. "Amory —get it!"

The tank slowed and stopped. Amory traversed the cannon until it was aimed low at the building and he pumped two H-E shells into it, followed by a pair of A-P shells. The wooden structure began to burn and the men who came out were cut down by the machine guns. Other tanks were firing at point-blank range at more buildings.

Ten of the Shermans were moving down the Main Street; the other six were mopping up along side streets. They were halfway to the assembly plants when a self-propelled 88 came lumbering toward them.

Dixon yelled a warning through the radio. Amory traversed his cannon fast, fired and missed. The 88 was in action as it stopped. German soldiers swarmed over the gun.

Carter rolled the tank off the street, over the sidewalk and crashed into one of the houses. The 88 roared. The second tank in the column died in its tracks. Dixon rotated the periscope to watch two of the crew open the main hatch and start to climb out. A man in civilian clothes had a rifle. He shot the first crewman. The second hit the street and began running. Two Germans darted out of a building, clubbed him to the sidewalk, and one raised a knife. Dixon's lips tightened.

The 88 was loading for another shot, but one of the tanks on a side street, got a perfect aim at the gun and smashed it with one H-E shell. The procession moved forward again. One tank pushed the burning victim of the 88 out of the way.

Dixon's tank backed out of the building into which it had crashed, rolled down the street slowly. Its machine gun fired at one side of the street, other tanks were taking care of the other side, and the cannons sent shells ripping into the buildings.

Everything seemed to be burning, except in the region where the factories were located. Dixon asked Carter for more speed and to head for the structures. Monda rested a moment and Amory held his fire for the assembly plants.

As they clanked and trundled toward the buildings, a man suddenly popped out of one of the large rolling doors waving a white sheet.

Hagen called over the network, "Hold fire! Hold everything!"

His tank moved up to the man. Hagen raised the hatch and lifted his head and shoulders out of the turret.

"We surrender," the man with the white sheet screeched. "We cannot fight!"

"Two minutes for everyone to get out of those buildings." Hagen said in his fair German. "I want the mayor of this town here two minutes after that."

Hagen consulted his watch as the man raced back to the buildings screaming the ultimatum. Workers came out in streams. Some were in uniform, most were not. Hagen directed six tanks to space themselves, train their guns on the buildings and stand ready. When the sweep-second hand of his watch ticked off two minutes, he gave the word to open up.

The machine guns fired incendiaries into the buildings and the cannon gutted them with both types of shells. In five minutes the half dozen long structures were burning furiously. Suddenly there were great explosions and whole sections of the buildings were blown upward and outward. The destruction was complete.

Hagen raised the hatch again and this time he climbed all the way out, holding his machine pistol ready. Under his orders, given through the throat mike, the tank turned around and rolled slowly toward a group of men with their arms raised high, except for a fat little man who was trying to tie a red sash over his shoulder while he nervously eyed the guns trained on him.

Hagen said, through the mike, "I'm getting down. If anyone takes a shot at me, level the town. Take your orders from Sergeant Dixon.

Dixon ripped the mike from his throat, opened the hatch, crawled out and jumped to the ground. His tank was behind the delegation which Hagen was now approaching. Machine guns covered the few people on the street, cowing them. There was little to worry about at the other end of the long Main Street, for everything was burning.

Hagen addressed the Mayor, who had finally gotten the red sash in place.

"This city is now surrendered to the American Army. All citizens will come from their homes unarmed and assemble here. You have five minutes."

There were, Hagen guessed, about four hundred people including a few children and about fifty military personnel.

"All of you," Hagen ordered, "will march into the West field. That is now delegated as an internment center. *Raus.*"

They began to mill toward the open field. Their faces were alight in horror and consternation. They knew about the treatment German tankers rendered a subdued city and they expected to be shot down.

Hagen turned his tanks loose on what was left of the town. He was in a hurry now, because alarms must be flashing all over this part of the country.

Dixon's tank moved to the end of the street to cover it. When the tank stopped, Carter threw open the hatch protecting his driver's seat and surveyed the wreckage with vast satisfaction.

Sal Monda scrambled down off the tank and

162

joined Dixon. They were outside the town hall, so far undamaged. Dixon eyed it suspiciously. He caught Hagen's eye, motioned toward the building and indictated he was going to search it. Hagen waved agreement.

"Come on," Dixon told Monda. "Let's see if there are any papers that might interest us."

They kicked open the door and looked down a long corridor. Nothing moved. Dixon started trotting down it. Sal Monda turned into the doorway of a large office. It seemed to be empty. He stopped inside.

A fury of arms, legs and skirts flew at him. The girl held a pocket knife in her hand and slashed at his face, cutting it in an arc down the right cheek.

Monda howled in pain, raised his rifle, but he didn't shoot. The girl was backed up against the wall, her tremendous fury replaced with terror. Monda looked her up and down. She was young, not more than twenty. A lush creature with a creamy complexion, big eyes, curving breasts and nice legs.

Monda blotted at the blood streaming from his check. He laid the gun down on a desk, walked slowly toward the girl and suddenly seized her. He drew her to him, kissing her, spilling his own blood over her face and shoulders.

He inserted a leg between hers, tripped her to the floor and fell upon her. She screamed and tried to cross her legs. He pried them apart with his knee. He pinned her down with a hand at her throat while he tore her dress almost off and then ripped at her panties. He got his pants open, threw himself on her and less than a minute it was over.

He got up, zipped the fly, picked up his rifle. The

girl managed to sit up. She was crying. Monda glared down at her, wiping away the blood on his face. She raised her head and looked at him. There were tears streaming down her cheeks.

Monda stared. He was no longer conscious of the fact that he was bleeding and that the girl had inflicted the wound. He said, "I'm sorry. I'm sorry . . . honest . . . sorry. I wish I hadn't done it. I'm sorry . . ."

She covered her face and sobbed bitterly. Monda heard Dixon yelling his name. He backed to the door. For an instant he considered shooting her. That might rid him of the picture of this violated girl, huddled on the floor, half naked, raped and beaten.

"Sal, where the hell are you?"

"Comin'," he called back. "Comin', Sarge."

He reached the door. The girl looked up again.

"I can't speak German and maybe you don't know what the hell I'm sayin', but I am sorry. Very sorry . . . I figured if you Krauts could do it to other people, I could do it too, but it ain't the same. That makes me sorry . . ."

He choked off the last word, stepped out and closed the door. Dixon was yelling for him.

"We're gonna blow this building," he said, "and move out. Come on, let's go."

"Hold it," Sal yelled. "Hold it a second . . ."

He rushed back into the room. The girl was on her feet. She screamed when she saw him and tried to reach the door, but he grabbed her arm, swung her out of the room into the corridor. Then, still holding her firmly, he half dragged her out of the building. She saw the tanks ready to fire. She turned her gaze on Sal and understanding flooded her eyes.

She reached up and touched his bleeding cheek gently. Then she laid her head against his blood-soaked battle jacket.

"Get the hell outa here," Sal cried. "Go on . . . *Raus!* Beat it! Over there!"

He pointed toward the field where everyone else in town was assembled. The girl nodded, held her torn dress together the best she could, and fled. At the end of the street, before she disappeared from view, she looked back at Sal. He was watching her. He half raised his hand in a salute, but he knew others were watching him. He growled a curse and ran to his tank. Dixon helped him aboard, noting his cut face but not commenting. Dixon hauled himself up too, slid through the hatch, clamped it down and gave orders to back away.

Six tanks fired at the town hall. One salvo gutted it and left it burning violently. Hagen's tank was already leaving. The others turned to follow. Fifteen tanks made it. The sixteenth was burning as they passed it. Two American tankmen lay sprawled on the street and sidewalk. Three others were inside the wrecked vehicle and none questioned they were dead.

They reached the road back. Hagen called for maximum speed and the column rolled away, leaving behind it a thoroughly demolished town. The Germans had a taste of the war they'd begun. Hagen hoped they enjoyed it and would realize it was only a small part of what was coming at them soon.

He led the column over the bridge and the spare tank crew hastily boarded a cargo carrier and fell in behind the tanks. Once clear of the bridge, it stopped long enough for the crew to dismount and set the fuses. Then the truck moved toward the formation again.

The bridge blew perfectly. The two German sentries were still sitting on a roadside bank, watching it all, still keeping their hands clasped behind their heads.

Hagen spoke over the network radio. "I want to offer each of you my sincerest thanks and congratulations. We gave them pure hell and a lot of it. We lost only one tank and its crew, but we did a million dollars worth of damage to that town. Those people know what they're in for now. The word will get around, all over Germany. If the news slows them just a little, we accomplished more than a million dollars worth of damage."

He paused to let his message sink in. Then he spoke with less enthusiasm.

"We're a hell of a long way from home and we're bound to be cut off. We'll be hit by everything they can bring up and planes will find us soon. We remain in formation until we're spotted. If only by observation planes, stay put. If Stukas or rocket-firing pursuits come in, spread out. Keep on the move. Two miles ahead is a forest. I noticed it on our way here. We'll stop there to refuel and rearm from the trucks. We do that as fast as humanly possible."

The tanks headed into the forest. There was no time to put up camouflage. They had to depend on either the excitement, or haste of the German spotters to overlook this place. There wasn't much hope they would, but the tanks must be refueled and armed.

Men piled out of them hastily, all except those in

166

Dixon's. Amory hoisted Sal Monda's limp body out of the hatch. Dixon grabbed him, eased him down.

"Somebody sliced him good," he said. "Break out the first-aid kit. And there's a bottle of cognac stashed away under my seat. Bring it. Hop!"

Dixon dusted sulpha powder into the gash on Monda's face, then he applied a heavy compress, bandaged him as well as he could while his men hastily filled the fuel tanks and passed shells and machine gun ammo into the tank.

Sal opened his eyes. Suddenly he began to cry.

"Take it easy, kid," Dixon said. "We got you fixed up okay. It's not bad."

"I wish I'd die. I wish they'd killed me. I shouldn'a done that. I shouldn'a done it . . ."

"What? What's eating you, kid?"

"I shouldn'a done it . . . I'm no goddamn good. No good . . . that's what's the matter with me."

Dixon hoisted him to his feet. "Listen, whatever's bothering you, forget it. We got a long way to go, right smack down the middle of a shooting gallery. Now get aboard before I boot you up there."

Sal climbed onto the tank and disappeared inside. He was ready to take the rest of the shells passed to him.

Twenty minutes were required for this operation. Then Hagen ordered all tanks on the move. The three cargo carriers were put out of action with grenades.

"All tanks move out," he commanded over the network radio. "Good luck!"

Dixon slammed the hatch and talked through the intercom to Carter, at the wheel.

"Rod, keep your eye on the Colonel's tank and stay as close to it as you can. If we have to disperse, stay with it. We got to get him back."

"I thought you hated his lousy guts," Carter said.

"That's got nothing to do with it. The guy just proved the theories he's been trying to put over for years. And don't forget this—I been helping him all them years, too. Or most of 'em. We got to get him back so he can explain all this and throw in the convincer that'll make the brass accept his views. Got that? We get him back or we don't go back ourselves."

FOURTEEN

THEY HIT the road and picked up speed. There was no percentage in crossing fields now, for they'd be seen wherever they were. Speed was the main factor and Shermans were built for it. They'd been made purposely light, sacrificing armor for better maneuverability. Their three inches of steel were small protection against the 88 *kanone* of the Tiger I, less than that when they faced the powerful armor-piercing shells fired by the Tiger II.

Faced with these, the only thing the Shermans could do was try to outrun them. Many military experts had urged heavier tanks, with more firepower, and some were supposed to be on the way, but that did the Strike Force little good.

Hagen had been one of those recommending heavier armor and more firepower and his wisdom and knowhow were amply proven by the fact that such tanks were sorely needed at once—and they weren't here.

The highway, two cars wide but of fairly good concrete construction, stretched out ahead of them. They had a long way to go. Dixon was developing the idea not many of them were going to make it.

They'd done a maximum amount of damage though, if anyone could find any solace in that, and they'd lost only one tank. But the Stuka raid had cut their forces almost in half. Another like that, this far behind the lines, and they were finished. A tank can't outrun a dive bomber, or a rocket, or bomb. It can only hide, so Dixon moved his scope around to keep forests or ravines within sight, if there were any to see.

The periscope gave unsatisfactory results, however, so he opened the hatch and sat with his head and shoulders above it. This was going to be a fine day. Damn it, he thought, why couldn't it be overcast, foggy, even rainy, so enemy planes wouldn't be in the sky?

But it was blue overhead, the fields and road bathed in bright sunlight. Dixon kept swiveling his head around to keep watch for planes.

What if this was a force of five hundred tanks now? With self-propelled guns, halftracks with mortars and anti-aircraft. Fuel trucks, carriers with plenty of ammo. Then they'd be something. They could take care of themselves. A force of such tremendous firepower could go almost anywhere.

Hagen used to talk it up, but very few would listen and Dixon really didn't blame them. Who could have foreseen a war fought with such mobility?

Patton was proving it in his own way by crashing on ahead and to hell with his flanks. Keeping on the move . . . always going forward, never stopping to defend or rest. There was always trouble ahead and Patton kept looking for it. He was ready to jump off now, only lacking supplies and fuel. Given all he needed, Dixon hardly doubted but that Patton could smash his way so deep into Germany, the Krauts would begin to consider surrender.

Their cities were already being plastered by bombs, but the terror of tank attack was even greater. Still, Patton's front was limited and there were other divisions and armies too. When the armor was ordered forward, everything else would be on the move. Dixon had long ago stopped questioning the decisions of his superiors.

They might as well have been on a routine peace-time patrol for they saw no one. There was no villages along this route for miles. Traffic was completely absent, a warning that there was danger.

"Blue Fox One to all commanders." The radio crackled with Hagen's voice. "The nearest air base from which the Germans can operate should put their planes in the air above us in a few minutes. We're going to catch hell. When I give the signal to disperse, every tank will put as much space between itself and its neighbor as possible. Head for any protection offered and do not attempt to defend yourself with ineffective fire. Your only chance is to evade. I wish all of you the best of luck."

Dixon raised his binoculars to his eyes and began a steady sky vigil. Dixon's was the last tank in the line, but he could see Hagen clearly, doing the same thing. Head tilted back, helmet off, graying hair picking up sunlight, giving it a silvery sheen.

Dixon passed a hand over his baldness and sighed. They were getting old all right. Two retreads fighting in a war that the youngsters could hardly withstand. Either of them could have remained home without any question of their courage arising. Both would have been invaluable in training, but they'd demanded to be shipped out and here they were.

Dixon rubbed his grease-and-dirt-smeared face vigorously, as if he were waking up. He was suddenly realizing that he didn't hate Luke Hagen any more. Maybe it was because what had happened was far, far back in their lives. Perhaps the reason lay in the fact that they were so much alike or—it could be that once he'd unburdened himself to Guillaine, his hatred began to subside.

He could even laugh at himself for thinking he'd ever had a chance with Guillaine. Even if there'd been no Colonel Hagen, Dixon was sadly outclassed by the French woman. And it occurred to him that he'd mistakenly believed he was in love with her simply because that was an expression of his hatred for Hagen.

Whatever it was, he realized that he didn't dislike Hagen any more and he wished he could tell him so. There seemed to be an impelling reason why he should, but Dixon couldn't sort out that reason from the several which occurred to him.

It wasn't until a few seconds before he sighted the planes that he knew the reason. In all likelihood they were both going to be killed during the next few minutes. Or, at least, one of them would get it. As much Dixon had wanted to unburden himself of the reason for his former hatred of the Colonel, he now wanted even more badly to tell him he was sorry—before it was too late.

There wasn't going to be time. The planes were coming in fast, pursuit jobs to machine gun them, maybe drop fire rockets, or a few light bombs and then keep them in sight until the Stukas and the heavies came along. Dixon had no doubt they'd employ all the planes they could round up.

Hagen's voice came over the network radio. "Blue Fox to all Commanders. Disperse! Disperse!"

Dixon took one final look at the oncoming planes, trying to count them. He estimated about a dozen, just the forerunner of what would soon follow up their attack. He slid down, slammed the hatch, strapped his helmet on and spoke over the intercom.

"Here they come, boys. Rod . . . there's no cover. Everybody else is veering off into the fields, but I say stick to the road. We can't zigzag, but we can maintain this high speed and that's worth something."

"Nobody else wants the goddamn road, we'll take it," Rod replied. "I'm in high now. Once we top the next grade, we'll have a nice long downhill slope. If they don't get us, we'll make time."

Now the land seemed to explode. What sounded like hail rattled against the sides of the tank. Some-

172

thing with the force of a meteor slammed against the main hatch cover, making Dixon's ears ring from the crash of sound.

It was now impossible to speak, even over the intercom. Dixon peered through the periscope. There was a black plume of smoke to the left, a quarter of a mile off the road and to the rear. That would be one of the tanks burning already. While he watched, a fighter came in low, its pilot knowing very well these tanks were unable to defend themselves from air attack. He fired a rocket at the same burning tank and the smoke changed to a lighter color for a moment, then dark again, and shot through with fire.

"The hell with this," Dixon shouted to nobody. He opened the hatch and raised himself high enough to observe. The sky was full of planes, darting in and out, banking, coming in low, machine guns throwing steel. For all this concentrated attack, there seemed to be only one tank dead and burning. The others were trundling along, making sudden turns, using the tactics they'd been taught.

Dixon kept his eyes on the fighters. If one turned his way, he meant to dive fast, but they'd already picked their targets and each plane seemed to have selected one tank as his special prey. After all, what did they have to worry about? Those they didn't get, the Stukas would smear and if they missed any, the heavies would drop their blockbusters under which nothing could survive.

Suddenly the planes broke off. Apparently they'd run out of ammo and rockets and bombs. They streaked off to the West and there were a few moments of comparative calm, during which Dixon saw one tank wobble and slow. It was to his right, about a hundred yards and it had been hit. One side of it was blackened from the explosion and it was slipping its left tread.

The hatch opened and the commander waved to Dixon, indicating that he was disabled. Dixon pressed the throat mike and gave Carter orders.

"Bear right. Kolosky's in trouble. We're going to pick up the crew."

"Roger," Carter said, and the tank swerved off the road onto the softer earth of the field and ran straight up beside the crippled tank.

"Climb on," Dixon yelled. "Everybody on!"

The commander leaped off the tank, and each crewman in turn came out of the hatch and jumped clear. The last one dropped a grenade down the turret before he jumped.

They clambered onto the back of Dixon's tank, signaled they were okay.

"Move out," Dixon ordered and Carter rolled the tank back to the highway where it gained fifteen miles an hour of speed. Kolosky crawled up to the top of the tank where he could speak to Dixon.

"How's it look, Sarge?"

"We're still due for the real pasting. It'll be here soon. When the Stukas come, I suggest you and the boys take a running dive on your bellies and stay flat. They might not spot you and your chances against their bombs are good."

"Yeah . . . I already gave the order, but we don't jump until the last minute. I feel a hell of a lot safer hanging onto this tank than digging a hole in the ground."

Dixon scanned the sky again. Hagen was out of the tank too, busy with the same chore. So far there'd been an interlude of about three or four minutes. Hell was arriving fast.

They came out of the south, heading toward the tanks, ready to smear them coming in before they made their turns and headed back to dish out more of the same. Some were pursuit craft.

"Wow!" Kolosky yelled. "There must be twenty or thirty of 'em."

"Take a powder," Dixon yelled. "While you still have a chance."

As he spoke, Dixon heard the first screeching dive of a Stuka and the firing of its machine guns. He looked up to see the nose of the dive bomber streaking toward the tank. It plummeted down, growing larger and larger.

"Evade," Dixon said over the intercom.

Kolosky and his crew jumped. The dive bomber caught two of them, flattening them before it raised its nose after the bomb release. The other three men were racing out into the field. A fighter came down in a graceful sweep, guns spitting viciously. All three men fell.

The Stuka bomb hit the road where the tank had been ten seconds before. Dirt, cement, stones flew upward and outward, hammering the tank. Dixon slid down until the rain of debris ceased. The tank was still moving. It had been fairly close, but only a direct hit was going to count. If it came, there'd be just one split second of horrible violence and then it would be over for tank and men.

From his position deep in the hatch, Dixon saw

another Stuka begin its dive. He pressed the throat mike hard. "Bear left . . . left . . . here comes another one. Left . . . more . . . more . . ."

The bomber pulled up as its bomb was released. It hit two hundred yards behind the tank. Dixon raised himself again, watching for those fighters. There seemed to be half a dozen mixed in with the Stukas. They were harder to anticipate than the dive bombers because the Stuka pilots had to aim their ships at the target they'd selected.

The whole area seemed to be exploding. The shriek of the bombers, added to the din of the guns, and the bomb explosions were like a madman's conception of hell.

Another Stuka had picked out Dixon's tank. This time Dixon waited only long enough to be sure he was the target. He slid down, slammed the hatch and braced himself. He hadn't liked the direction of the dive. It seemed to be just about perfect.

In a few seconds the bomb would be released. "Bear right," he yelled through the intercom. Carter heard him without the earphone. He brought the tank about as quickly as the monster could move. Carter began to count. One thing about being buttoned up, you couldn't hear the damned screaming plane.

There was a blast and the tank seemed to have been picked up by a wave, held aloft, and then dropped violently down. Everything loose set up a terrific rattle. Sal Monda cried out in pain. Probably his already aching face had been smashed against some object. Then the treads gripped, the tank moved on.

As Dixon saw it, this was the middle of the attack. First the fighters, now the Stukas, and finally they'd send in the heavies. Dixon estimated that the Stukas were the worst. The heavies, if they hit anywhere close by, would be the greater destroyers, but even the best of bombers had a hard time dropping their sticks smack on a moving, zig-zagging target.

Not that they wouldn't get some of the tanks. They'd saturate the field with bombs and they were bound to inflict death and damage.

Dixon scanned the area through his periscope. He grimly counted four dead and burning tanks. That made five crippled, eleven remaining, and the attack was not yet half over.

"Get back on the highway," Dixon ordered. "We hit the rise in a minute and then we'll pick up speed. There may be some kind of protection over the hill."

A bomb struck fairly close by, making the tank shake violently, but she maintained her speed. Amory angrily slapped the breech of his loaded 75 and cursed its ineffectiveness against the planes. He had an impelling urge to fire the gun anyway, just at the landscape. At least it would seem they were doing something other than waddling along as perfect targets for the practice runs of these pilots.

"What are they throwing at us?" Kiley asked, from his bow gunner's seat.

"Freight cars," Carter said. "Loaded with TNT."

Sal Monda was beginning to sob. The intercom was alive and Dixon joined in. "They got five of us, but we're still rolling. The Colonel's okay so far."

"They'll have to drop a locomotive on him," Kiley said. "Hey, Sarge, you got anything left in that bottle you stashed away?"

Dixon had forgotten it. He reached around and found it intact. He pulled the cork, took a drink, handed it down to Kiley and it made its way through the crew, with only Monda passing it up.

"I can't open my mouth," he said thickly. "I'm hurt bad. I gotta have a doctor."

"Sure . . ." Carter said unfeelingly. "We'll put in a phone call right now. How the hell did you get cut that way anyhow?"

"He musta grabbed a *fraulein* and she had long fingernails," Amory said, almost hitting the truth.

"You can all go to hell," Monda said. "I'm hurt and you guys just laugh."

Dixon said, "Listen, Sal, just beyond three inches of armor that's keeping you alive, are five burning tanks with their crews roasting. And you have a gripe? Get with it, kid."

Monda muttered something unintelligible. Dixon wasn't paying any attention. He was listening, trying to figure out what was happening in the sky above them. There'd been no more jarring explosions. They were moving up the slope toward the top. In a few seconds they'd nose down and move faster. The more speed, the better their chances of avoiding bombs.

He pressed his face against the periscope. They were at the top. Below, perhaps half a mile away, was a thick grove of trees. They looked as inviting as an oasis on the desert. Dixon pushed the mike against his throat.

"Rod . . . see that grove?"

"Yeah . . . it sure looks good, Sarge."

"Had for it. Maybe we can roll into it before the

178

heavies or more Stukas come. It's our best bet. Step on it."

"I got this thing open wide. What the hell do you think it is, a racing car?"

Dixon raised the hatch and himself, for a quick look around. The remaining tanks were spread out, no longer performing their dance of evasion, but crawling along as fast as possible. Hagen was heading toward the highway, to adopt Dixon's strategy of using speed rather than maneuverability. No doubt Hagen had also spotted the grove.

Miraculously, there were no planes in the sky. Like the eye of the hurricane, Dixon knew the calm was deceptive. At least cooling, fresh air circulated through the tank, reviving its groggy crew for a time. They were rolling well toward the grove. Five minutes more at the most. . . .

Then the distant sky was filled with them. Dixon guessed there were fighters, more Stukas and the heavies, all coming in waves. Somebody, maybe Goering himself, had ordered the *Luftwaffe* to get this strike force. Hitler would know about the raid and the invasion of the Reich very soon. Somebody had to stop his ranting with the news that the entire strike force had been wiped out. Nothing else would calm him down.

That was how Dixon figured it, purely for his own amusement. Actually, it was more likely that some obscure commander was throwing all this at the force as a matter of course.

The difference in who gave the command was nil. The tanks were now going to get a real pasting.

The planes were still far away. It would be a horse

race to see who won. The tank lumbering into the grove, or bombs falling on the tank. Dixon kept his glasses glued on the planes. He picked up the network radio mike.

There was no sense in using code this time. "Dixon to all tanks. Boogies comin' in, skyful! We're gonna dive into that grove of trees. Button up and hang on. It's gonna be bad."

Hagen's tank was frantically heading for the grove too. Once there, the tanks would be immobilized but, with luck, out of sight. The planes might gomb the whole grove, but they'd have no target and that was important. Tanks could survive near misses, they could plunge deeply into a forest and maybe ride out an attack like this. It was better than racing over the open terrain.

Dixon slid down, closed the hatch again and turned the periscope toward the grove. Nothing else mattered now, just that thick forest of trees. They meant life.

Suddenly the tank sang with the impact of machinegun bullets. Why the pilots insisted on machine gunning tanks was beyond Dixon's scope of imagination. None of their bullets were armor piercing.

The Stuka bombs were exploding and now there was something new added. Under the impact of the heavy bombs, the tank began to rock like a cradle, but with jerky movements that threatened to dump it on its side.

The whole earth was shuddering under the impact. There was a gigantic crashing sound and Dixon's heart stopped beating until he realized the tank was entering the grove, and the noise was caused as it bulldozed through the trees, taking some of them down in the process.

Carter was showing his skill now. Peering through the driver's slit, he gauged where the tank could go and where it might be stopped dead. He made one violent turn to the left, the blunt nose came up against a tree with a huge trunk. Dixon raised the hatch and ducked a branch that swung out with the hatch and bounced back to try and take his head off.

"Cut the engines," he ordered. "We don't want to make any exhaust smoke to show where we are."

The engines died and the sudden cessation of sound and vibration made them all feel uncomfortable, as if they'd been stripped naked and were now sitting ducks.

The bombs were crashing in salvos. Dixon stood up, but he could see nothing but trees. Without question the pilots knew at least one tank had rolled into the grove and they'd soon concentrate on it.

Dixon picked up the radio mike. "Dixon to all commanders. How are we doing? Repeat . . . how are we doing? Check in, please."

Nobody answered. Dixon felt that awful sinking sensation that comes when a man—or a tank crew—believes it's all alone in the middle of the attacking enemy. Dixon shut off the radio.

"You guys . . . nobody answers the radio. Maybe they all got it. I'm gonna go see. Anybody wants to come is welcome."

"Better'n sittin' here waitin' to get fried," Carter said. "Come, you guys, get out so I can climb up there."

Dixon jumped to the ground, followed by Kiley, then Amory and finally Carter.

"Where's Sal?" Dixon asked Carter.

"He's squatted down with his hands over his face. Kid's gone nuts, I think."

"The hell with him," Dixon said unfeelingly. "Let's go see what's happened."

The crunch of several heavies made Kiley wince. "Somebody must be alive out there for them to be bombing."

They reached the edge of the grove where the trees were smaller and sparse. Now they could look up through the thinning branches and see the sky. Only the heavies were left. The other planes had gone home, probably lacking fuel for any extended stay. Dixon carefully parted high brush and looked out over the sloping approach to the grove. The tanks had made the crest of the slope as the bombs fell. They were there now—four of them burning like a funeral pyre, five more dead where they stood, two tipped over. One seemed to have been hit from beneath, for it appeared to be standing on its nose.

The tank closest to Dixon was Hagen's. It was blackened, but it didn't seem to have been caught in a close blast. The hatch cover stood open.

Dixon said, "I'm going out. The rest of you stay here. That's an order if you ever heard one. If I don't get back, stay with the tank until the sky clears and then hightail it."

He freed himself of his binoculars and helmet and ran lightly out into the field. The bombers were

182

circling overhead. If he was spotted, they'd start bombing again. Those babies could linger up there for a long time.

Dixon reached the tank and dropped onto the ground alongside it.

"Hey," he called out, "any life in there?"

The driver's slit pulled back. "We're okay," the unseen driver said. "That you, Dixon?"

"Yeah, we made it to the grove. What happened?"

"Nothing. Hold it, Colonel's coming out, Sarge."

Dixon eyed the sky. The bombers were leaving. What was left of Strike Force was having a break at last. Dixon pounded on the side of the tank.

"It's okay . . . they've gone. It's okay."

Hagen popped out of the hatch, slid down the tank and joined him.

"They got a near miss with us and we stalled to make them think we were dead. I guess it worked."

"We're in the grove," Dixon said. "Okay too. But looks like everybody else got it."

"I know."

"We were expendable anyway. We gave 'em hell before they got us though. What'll we do now, pull out and take our chances again?"

"We better wait for darkness. I hope the *Luftwaffe* radioed back that they got us all. I don't think they saw you slip into the trees. At the time you were not under attack and there was a hell of a lot of smoke from those heavies. I think that saved both of us."

"Maybe you'd better hide out, too," Dixon said.

"I'll join you, Sergeant."

Dixon nodded and ran back to the grove.

"They okay?" Kiley asked.

"Yes . . . that's all though, just the Colonel's tank. We're going to hide out until dark . . ."

The whine of the starter on the Colonel's tank reached them. There seemed to be no response from the engines. Maybe the tank had died after all.

"Sure makin' a funny noise," Carter said, with the knowledgeable assurance of an expert. "Funny as hell . . . hey . . . that ain't the tank. There's another one . . . some place."

Dixon raced out into the clearing. From the highway behind the grove of trees, a Tiger II was lumbering toward Hagen's crippled tank. Dixon threw himself to the ground, rolled madly over and over until he reached the grove. Kiley helped him up. He'd seen the enemy tank too.

"*Alles kaput,*" Kiley said forlornly. "Hagen's got no chance!"

FIFTEEN

THE HUGE Tiger II left the highway and rolled onto the field, its long cannon traversing to cover one of the bombed tanks. The Tiger rolled closer, stopped. The hatch flew open and the commander gave his orders. The cannon belched and an armor-piercing shell smashed through the stalled Sherman.

The Tiger threw one more shell into it, backed off, and the commander ordered an attack on another of the disabled tanks. They shelled that one twice and then the Tiger moved toward Hagen's tank which stood dead, unable to defend itself against this monster which outgunned it.

Dixon said, "Let's go!"

They raced back to their tank and climbed aboard. Carter turned the tank around, drove it toward the cleared field. Dixon rode with the hatch open. Against this monster an open or closed hatch wasn't going to make any difference.

The Tiger waddled closer to Hagen's tank, but apparently the commander believed that, like the others, the tank and its crew were dead.

The Tiger's back was toward Dixon's Sherman. For some reason the German commander buttoned up so that, while his tank was in motion, he couldn't hear the Sherman coming up from behind.

Dixon said, "Amory, we got one chance. Put the first one right where that cannon is. If we can disable the gun, we've got 'em."

"Right," Amory said.

"Kiely, stand by the machine gun. The Krauts may come out flying or they may try to ram us. Either way, pour it on. All set? Then wait for the command."

Carter was moving the Sherman fast. If they were discovered and the Tiger II traversed its cannon toward them, everything was finished.

"Stand by," Dixon called. There seemed to be no

other tanks. Probably this one had been on patrol and ordered by radio to move in and clean up.

"Got 'em," Amory called over the intercom. "Right in my sights."

"Range two hundred. Hold it another few seconds. If the gun starts moving, let her rip."

But the Tiger was intent on Hagen's tank. Perhaps, in some manner, they guessed the tank wasn't dead. A disabled tank is usually battered and Hagen's was not. They were going to put an armor-piercing shell through it and make sure it was finished off.

"Fire," Dixon said.

The 75 blasted and the aim was good. It hit the tank on the left side, just at the base of its cannon. Sal Monda was working again. He threw another H-E into the tube, slammed the block closed. Amory fired and this shell hit the turret, glancing off it, but if the commander was inside that turret, he had loose teeth.

"Down," Dixon shouted. "Down . . . the treads."

Amory spun the cannon down. Sal had already loaded up. Amory drew a bead, fired. The Tiger was jolted by this one. It started to move, but the left tread had been warped, broken and shattered by the shell.

Amory threw more shells at the tank, aiming anywhere so long as he had a hit. The hatch flew open. Kiley let out a whoop and started firing bursts. His tracers showed how good his aim was. The man coming out of the turret fell over.

"Move in," Dixon ordered.

The Sherman waddled forward and at point-blank range began to pump shells at the Tiger. When the smoke cleared, it was sadly battered. Everyone inside had to be dead.

Colonel Hagen and his four men popped out of the Sherman and raced toward them. Dixon came out of his tank to lend a hand.

Hagen waved to him. "I'll ride outside. Let's go, in case that Tiger radioed for help."

"You belong inside, sir," Dixon said.

One of Hagen's crew suddenly let out a wild yell. The one thing no one expected, the machine gun turret on the Tiger was swinging toward them. By some slim chance, at least one of the Germans was alive and the turret still worked.

The gun chattered. Hagen fell off the tank, tried to get up, fell again. Amory fired a shell at the machine-gun turret, followed it up with three more as fast as Sal could load. The machine gun was now silent.

Dixon jumped to the ground, ran to where Hagen lay. The bullets had caught him high—three or four of them, probably through the shoulders and the top of the chest. Maybe . . . just maybe . . . they'd missed the lung area.

The crew was dead. They'd caught the full blast of the gun. Among them was Lieutenant Miller. It didn't matter now that he'd cracked. Dixon lifted Hagen to where Kiley waited. The Colonel was brought inside the tank. They moved out as soon as Dixon took a running jump, secured a grip on a hand-hold and clung to the tank as it rolled toward the road.

They made it back late that night. A radio message cleared the way, air cover came out to meet them and they rolled in safely. Twenty-five tanks had started out on this foray. One returned.

Dixon waited until he saw Colonel Hagen placed on a litter and carried to the field hospital. Then he reported to Intelligence and gave a detailed survey of what had happened. Before he was finished, he got word that Hagen's condition was fair. They were sending him to the rear by ambulance.

Dixon didn't reach the base-camp hospital for three days and when he got there, he felt as if he ought to check in as a patient instead of a visitor.

Shaven, bathed, wearing a clean uniform, Dixon felt like a new man except for the fatigue which he couldn't shake off. Sessions with Intelligence had been rugged and long. He pased up a drink with considerable effort because he wanted to be cold sober when he told Hagen their feud was off. That no matter what had happened fifteen years ago, they'd buried it forever after the foray of the strike force.

Guillaine came down the hospital corridor to where Dixon had been told to wait. She sat beside him on the bench.

"I left word that if you came, I was to see you first, Sergeant."

She looked more beautiful to him than ever.

"How is he? That's all I want to know. If he's too sick . . ."

"No . . . no, he is doing very well. He has refused to be sent back and the doctors have already agreed he will be fit for duty again in a few weeks. He is coming to my chalet to recuperate."

"Okay, that's great. I couldn't wish anything better for him. Now I want to apologize . . ."

"Yes," she said, "you should. You were very coarse and very drunk that night. That is why I am going to tell you the truth about this incident fifteen years ago. Luke has told me, but he does not wish you to know. I do—because I don't believe you will ever let yourself forget and always, your blame and hatred goes to him."

"But I said . . ."

"Be quiet, Sergeant. You deserve this. Luke did not kill your wife and his that day. He did his best to stop them and your wife did her best to crash into his car and send it over the cliff. She failed and went over herself. The brake marks were from Luke's car as he did his best to stop them from going over."

Dixon nodded slowly. "One of the Highway Patrol officers said he figured something like that could have happened, but me, I wouldn't believe it. I . . ."

"You will remain silent another moment, please. You were not in love with me. You knew Luke was and you told yourself he was taking me away from you. Is that not so?"

He nodded. "Look, I want to forget the whole thing . . ."

"One small additional matter and you may forget it—if you can. Your wife was not helping the Colonel's wife run away from him. He never abused her. She lied and so did your wonderful Lois. Do you want to know the truth, Sergeant? Your wife had become a Lesbian. Luke's wife was under her influ-

ence. They were not running away. They were elop-
ing."

"What kind of talk . . ." he began, and then his
mind switched back abruptly to fifteen years ago, to
the change which he'd seen and felt come over Lois.
She'd never been an ardent woman at love-making,
but then she'd turned absolutely cold, even uncom-
municative toward him and there'd been no reason for
it.

Dixon remembered her strange absences from home
overnight which she told him were because she had
to be with some girl friend who was ill. And when he
finally did check up on her, he found it to be true.
She had spent the night at some girl friend's home and
he saw nothing wrong in that.

Now, fifteen years later, he refused to accept
Guillaine's story.

"I don't believe it," he said, "and how can you
when there's no proof?"

"You accepted Luke Hagen's guilt when there was
no proof," she reminded him. "You were pleased
when his military career was stopped. I am very
angry with you, Sergeant. You hated the man who en-
dured your hatred and the loss of promotion simply
because he did not wish you to learn the ugly truth
about your wife."

"But she and Alicia . . ." Dixon shook his head.
The Colonel's wife had seemed like such a lady and
had been so in love with him. But then . . . now
that he thought back . . . she and Lois had spent a
great deal of time together and, according to army
protocol, a colonel's lady and a sergeant's wife were
rarely that close.

"I might also add," Guillaine said, "that there is proof. A letter Luke's wife left and which no one has ever seen except me. Even now he does not know I tell you this. He may be angry with me, but I could not let your hatred go on and I want to see that Luke is rewarded as a good soldier should be—by promotion."

"Can you show me the letter?"

"It is in my handbag—in his room. I will bring it to you at once."

She was gone only a few minutes while Dixon paced the corridor, facing up to this sudden change in the situation far better than he'd expected, just after the impact of the truth hit him. And now he knew it was the truth.

When she returned and handed him the envelope, he read the letter quickly and then tucked it in the pocket of his jacket.

"You must not keep the letter," she protested. "I trusted you in letting you see it . . ."

"Trouble is, Guillaine, the Colonel's got no more sense than me. You're the only one using your head. I'll see he gets it back, but first it's going to Washington. The Colonel has rated a star for a long time. I've been fathead enough to be happy he never advanced, but now he's going to get his star if I have to go right to the head of SHAEF."

She reached out her hand. "Thank you, Bert. I could not ask you to do this, you know."

"I'll be back when I've got it settled. I don't want to see him until then. Luke's the kind of a guy you have to look in the eye and I couldn't . . . until everything is cleared. Thanks for telling me."

Dixon stepped out into the sunlight. The letter made a crackling sound in his breast pocket as he strode briskly toward the building with the staff car in front of it. The two star flag on the car hung limply.

He walked into the beginning of the pipeline that led directly to the War Department in Washington.